"So," Daniel said, "you and Jeremy must be getting pretty serious if you were willing to give up an extra half hour of sleep just to surprise him."

Jade stiffened, wondering why everyone suddenly had to use that word—*serious*.

"We're *not* getting serious," she insisted.

What was wrong with her? Since when did she care what other people thought, especially a guy she barely knew and had only worked with for, like, two seconds? *Since never*, she told herself, exhaling sharply and giving Daniel a quick wave before turning to leave.

Sure, Jade had bought Jeremy a present, and she had gotten up extra early to deliver it—which was totally against her nature—but half the reason she had done it in the first place was because she knew how uptight Jessica would get when she saw Jeremy unwrapping the adorable, tiny stuffed dog with the little thank-you heart Jade had stuck to one of its ears. Not exactly the motive of a devoted girlfriend.

So what if she actually enjoyed doing something nice for Jeremy? He was a nice guy, and she liked him. That's all there was to it. Daniel could believe whatever he wanted.

Don't miss any of the books in SWEET VALLEY HIGH
SENIOR YEAR, an exciting series from Bantam Books!

Visit the Official Sweet Valley Web Site on the Internet at:

www.sweetvalley.com

Francine Pascal's SVH senioryear

So Not Me

CREATED BY
FRANCINE PASCAL

BANTAM BOOKS
NEW YORK • TORONTO • LONDON • SYDNEY • AUCKLAND

RL: 6, AGES 012 AND UP

SO NOT ME

A Bantam Book / October 2000

Sweet Valley High® is a registered trademark of Francine Pascal.
Conceived by Francine Pascal.
Cover photography by Michael Segal.

Copyright © 2000 by Francine Pascal.
Cover art copyright © 2000 by 17th Street Productions,
an Alloy Online, Inc. company.

Produced by 17th Street Productions,
an Alloy Online, Inc. company.
33 West 17th Street
New York, NY 10011.

ISBN: 0-553-49338-8

Visit us on the Web! www.randomhouse.com/teens

Published simultaneously in the United States and Canada

Bantam Books is an imprint of Random House Children's Books, a
division of Random House, Inc. BANTAM BOOKS and the rooster
colophon are registered trademarks of Random House, Inc. Bantam Books,
1540 Broadway, New York, New York 10036.

PRINTED IN THE UNITED STATES OF AMERICA

OPM   0 9 8 7 6 5 4 3 2 1

To Miriam Ribner

Jade Wu

I'm so sick of those lame headlines they put on the front of women's magazines, like "How to Drive Your Guy Wild" or "Ten Surefire Ways to Keep Your Boyfriend Interested." And all those love quizzes? They're even worse. As if there's actually such a thing as "true love." Yeah, it always seems perfect in the beginning, and then it gets boring, and someone leaves—usually the guy. That's why it's stupid for girls to get attached and start scheduling their lives around their boyfriends. Why bother when it's just going to end eventually anyway? There's no way I'd trade my freedom for the whole girlfriend-boyfriend thing.

Okay, maybe Jeremy's not like most guys out there. I guess I could sort of see us together for a while. But not a <u>long</u> time. I could never do that.

Well, I hate using the word <u>never</u>. It won't happen, though. Um, probably not.

Jeremy Aames

First it was Jessica. I totally fell for her, and just when I thought things were going great, she dumped me for Will Simmons. Then I met Jade. Same thing. It seemed like everything was falling into place until I saw her kissing some other Sweet Valley jock.

I'm pretty much over that now—I mean, Jade explained what was actually going on, and it's obvious she feels really bad. But still, I'm kind of starting to think that Jade's whole carefree thing is really the right idea. I mean, life is supposed to be fun, right? And if you take it too seriously, it's just one letdown after another. So maybe it's time I lightened up a little.

Conner McDermott

What. The. Hell.

CHAPTER

Boiling Point

Conner McDermott stared around his living room in shock, still trying to absorb the sight of every one of his friends, his mom, and his sister, Megan, all there in front of him.

Elizabeth sat between Evan and Megan on the sofa, and Tia, Andy, and Maria were squeezed together on the matching love seat. His mother was perched on the edge of the sofa beside Elizabeth, watching him. Well, they were *all* watching him, actually. But it was his sister's gaze that really got him—she was looking at him with this horrible mixture of pain and fear. He'd seen that expression on her face before but never directed at him.

Conner glanced back at Elizabeth, barely able to believe the words that had just come out of her mouth. *Conner, we're here because we love you.* He clenched his hands into tight fists at his sides, wondering if this was all just some really sick joke.

No one else had spoken since Elizabeth's little declaration, and he was waiting to see what would come next, his feet practically glued to the floor.

1

"It's about your drinking," Tia finally said.

His entire body went rigid as he moved his gaze to his supposed best friend. Tia kept her wide, brown eyes focused on his face without flinching, but he knew her well enough to recognize the slight tremble in her lips that always came when she was trying to hide her emotions.

Megan let out a small, choked noise, and the anger that had been building inside him since he walked in the house reached the boiling point. How could they have dragged Sandy into this? He could never forgive them—not a single one of the other people in this room.

Suddenly whatever had been holding him here released its grip, and Conner whirled around and stormed toward the front door. He didn't even feel the sting as his shoulder clipped the wall on his way out. He shoved open the door, reaching into his pocket with his other hand for the keys to his Mustang. His fingers tightened around the jangling metal. Just a few feet more and he'd be behind the wheel.

"Conner! Wait!" Tia yelled. Her footsteps came thudding after him, but he didn't turn back. Instead he quickened his pace and yanked open his car door, then slid into the driver's seat and shut the door. Just as he jammed his keys into the ignition, Tia appeared at his open window.

"Look—I know you're mad," she said. The wind

blew her long, dark hair out from her face in every direction. "But I'm not going to just let you leave. I can't stand by and watch you do this to yourself." Conner stared back at her for a second, flexing his jaw. "Please," she begged, tears starting to slide down her cheeks. "Please listen to us—to me."

The pathetically *desperate* tone of her voice only filled him with disgust. Why was everyone so bent on "saving" him anyway? Nothing was wrong with him! He put the car in reverse and hit the accelerator, jerking the car backward down the driveway. He whipped the Mustang out onto the road in a quick half circle that left dirt flying behind him. Checking his rearview mirror, he saw Tia chasing the car down the driveway, but he refused to even glance in her direction.

Not going to let me leave, huh? he thought, shifting into first. *Well, let's see you stop me.* Gripping the steering wheel so hard his knuckles turned white, he sped off.

"Can you tell what's happening?" Megan asked, standing on her toes in an attempt to peer around Mrs. Sandborn, Maria, and Andy. They were all clustered around the living-room window, with the blue drapes pushed back out of the way.

Conner's mom let out an audible breath. "It's hard to see from this angle," she said quietly. "But I think he's taking off."

Elizabeth tried to listen to what Mrs. Sandborn was saying, but it was as if they were in separate rooms. Nothing could drown out the sound of her own voice inside her head. *It's my fault,* she kept thinking. *I said the wrong thing. I didn't say enough. Or maybe I shouldn't have said anything...*

"Liz? Are you okay?" Evan asked, his voice somehow soft and near enough to penetrate. She glanced up and turned to meet his gaze, taking in the sympathy that filled his big, blue eyes.

Slowly Elizabeth shook her head. *Okay?* No, she wasn't. Not even close.

Evan leaned toward her, resting his elbows on his knees. "He's going to be okay," he promised. "And either way, you did everything you could."

She choked out a laugh. "Then I guess that's not much," she said. *She* should be out there right now, helping her boyfriend. Instead it was Tia. And only because she couldn't cut it, couldn't come through when Conner needed her most. "I just feel so *useless,*" she admitted, staring back down at her hands.

"Useless?" Evan echoed, sounding genuinely confused. "How could you say that?"

Elizabeth bit her lip, trying to keep from breaking down. That was the last thing Megan needed to see. But she couldn't stop the rush of pain, and she felt herself deflate, sinking against Evan. He put his arm around her shoulders and gave her a gentle squeeze.

4

The front door banged shut, and Elizabeth's head jerked up. Within seconds Tia came into the room—alone. She shook her head, and Elizabeth's stomach seemed to cave in on itself.

He's gone. She swallowed. *He's gone, and it's my fault.*

Jade leaned back against the torn sofa cushion, surveying her living room with a satisfied smile. Her heart rate was still slightly accelerated even though Jeremy had left over half an hour ago. *Now, that was a kiss,* she thought, recalling their twenty-minute make-out session. The guy was a natural.

The sound of the front doorknob rattling, followed by jingling keys, caught Jade's attention. She listened for voices, wondering if her mom was alone or with her newest boyfriend, Jim. *Or is it Tim?*

"I'm home," Ms. Wu called out as she pushed open the door, two bags of groceries in one arm and a bouquet of flowers cradled in the other. Jade jumped up and ran over to grab the bags of food. She glanced out into the courtyard of the apartment development, happy to see that Jim—or Tim—wasn't in the vicinity.

After Jade and her mom had set the flowers and groceries down in the kitchen, Jade shot her mom a teasing look. "Secret admirer?" she asked, waving her hand at the flowers.

Ms. Wu laughed. "Not this time," she said,

hanging her purse over the back of one of the kitchen chairs. She leaned over to smell the flowers. "Mmmm. They're really nice," she said, her dark eyes twinkling. "I just picked them up for the two of us," she continued, walking over to the sink and removing the flowers' plastic sleeve. "I thought we deserved a little gift."

Jade shook her head. Her mom was always doing stuff like that—little, thoughtful gestures.

She watched while her mom cut the stems, throwing the clippings into the big plastic trash can on the other side of the sink. Ms. Wu's long, black hair was neatly pinned back in a low chignon, and her small, delicate hands moved swiftly. She finished what she was doing, then pulled down a glass vase from above the refrigerator to start arranging the flowers.

"The flowers are beautiful," Jade said as she began unpacking the rest of the groceries. "And it's perfect timing because we have something to celebrate." Ms. Wu immediately stopped fiddling with the flowers and turned to glance at Jade with raised eyebrows.

Jade grinned. "I'm seeing that guy again," she said. "The one I told you about."

Ms. Wu frowned. "What was his name? Josh Rolinsky?"

Jade rolled her eyes. "It's *Radinsky*, Mom—Josh Radinsky—but no, not him. Jeremy Aames. The guy

6

I worked with at House of Java." Was she actually blushing as she said his name? Not possible.

"Oh, right. I thought things didn't work out with him."

Jade shrugged. "Well, yeah. I mean, he was upset because he saw me hanging out with Josh at the beach, but that's all over now." She removed one last item from the paper bag—a jar of peanut butter—then collapsed the bag into a flat rectangle and stuffed it into the small space between the refrigerator and the oven.

"So everything's going well?" Ms. Wu asked, moving the roses from the counter to the center of the kitchen table. She pulled out a chair and sank down into it.

"Kind of." Jade hesitated. "I mean, it's not exclusive or anything, but last night I went over to his house, and we hung out with his sisters, Trisha and Emma—they were *so* cute, and you should have seen Jeremy with them—it was adorable. He's so sweet and—" She stopped, realizing that her mother was staring at her with a puzzled expression. "What?" she asked, sitting down in the chair across from her mom.

"It just doesn't sound like one of your usual dates," Ms. Wu said. "Playing with his sisters?"

Jade tugged at the sleeves of her shirt. "Yeah, I guess that is sort of a weird thing to do on a date, but it was actually kind of fun. Oh, and he stopped by a little while ago to tell me about this new sushi bar that's opening in town. His dad's friends with the manager, so he gave the guy my name and everything. Isn't that nice? Working there will probably be much better than House of Java anyway."

After all, Jessica Wakefield won't be my boss, she thought. Remembering the look on Princess Jessica's face when she'd told Jade she was fired still made her wince. And she'd been really freaked out over finding a new job until Jeremy came through for her today. He was pretty good at that whole being-there-when-you-needed-him thing.

Ms. Wu reached back and pulled her hair loose from the bun, running her fingers through it. "Was that the only reason Jeremy stopped by?" she asked. "Just to tell you about the job?"

"Not exactly," Jade hedged. She pressed her lips together, fully aware of what her mother was getting at. But there were some details she wouldn't share with her mom—no matter how close they were.

"Well," Ms. Wu said, leaning over to adjust the flowers once again, "it sounds like things are getting serious."

Jade frowned. Serious? Because she spent one night with his sisters and then he helped her find a job? "What is that supposed to mean?" she asked.

Her mom shrugged. "I don't know. You're meeting his family; he's finding you jobs." She paused. "And usually you tell me things like what kind of car the guy drives or how he dresses, but this time you're saying how 'nice' and 'sweet' Jeremy is."

Jade shifted in her seat—could her mother possibly be more out of touch? Where was she coming up with all of this?

"Okay," she said, running her hands along the edge of the small table, "if you really need to know, Jeremy drives a beat-up old Mercedes, and he dresses like an ad for the Gap."

And he also happens to be very nice and incredibly sweet, she thought. So maybe he didn't fit her usual have-a-little-fun-then-ditch-him guy type. But that did *not* mean she was actually getting serious about Jeremy Aames.

"So that was a total failure, huh?" Tia said, slouching in the passenger seat of Andy's vintage Cadillac. Andy checked his rearview mirror quickly before flicking on his turn signal to change lanes.

"I don't know," he responded. "I mean, at least Conner knows that *we* all think he has a drinking problem now—even if he doesn't believe it himself." It was a lame attempt at comfort, especially considering what Tia had told him about how angry Conner was when he took off, but it was the best Andy could do right now.

"I guess," Tia agreed halfheartedly. She put her feet up on the dashboard, crossing them at the ankles.

"Hey," Andy said, nodding toward Tia's legs. "Watch the leather."

Tia glared at him. "It's plastic, Andy," she said, her voice sounding a little less empty and bleak.

"I prefer leatherette," Andy responded, mock indignant. Tia's mouth curved into a brief half smile before returning to its former frown. Oh, well—it was a start.

Noticing the few sprinkles of rain that were beginning to dot his windshield, Andy turned on his wipers. The back-and-forth squeaking motion against the glass seemed to accentuate the silence within the car.

In a way Andy envied Conner. Not the problem he had, definitely, but the fact that everyone around him *knew* and was trying to help. The few people Andy had told that he was gay had yet to show that they even cared, and Andy still hadn't managed to tell the people who really mattered—his parents. Watching Mrs. Sandborn today—the way she looked at Conner when he was in the room with them—he couldn't help thinking about his mom and how she'd react if he told her the truth.

If. Shouldn't it be when? He had to tell her sometime, right?

Andy shot a glance at Tia as he slowed down for the upcoming red light. Tia was staring vacantly out the passenger-side window, her expression totally blank. He knew this wasn't the best time to bring it up, but maybe Tia could actually use the distraction.

He cleared his throat. "Um, Tee," he started. "I've been thinking a lot about, you know, what I told you. About being gay." He paused, waiting for some sort of reaction, but her gaze was still focused out the window. Maybe she was just waiting for him to finish? "Anyway, I know I said I was okay with it before, but that's not totally true. I mean, there's still some stuff I have to work out." He took a deep breath. "Like if I should tell my parents." She still didn't move. "Tia?" he prompted, raising his voice.

Tia jumped slightly. "I'm sorry—what?" she asked, looking at him with confusion in her large, brown eyes. She obviously hadn't heard a single word of what he'd said. *It's okay,* Andy told himself. *I'll consider that a rehearsal.* He steeled himself and got ready to start over.

"So anyway," he started again, "I was thinking that maybe I should tell my parents—"

"About Conner's drinking?" Tia interrupted. "You mean they don't already know? I spilled everything to my mom and dad the other night after my brothers were in bed—I had to. I mean, they've known Conner since he was, like, three years old."

Andy felt a swell of frustration rising in his chest. Would it kill the girl to think about someone other than Conner for five seconds? He shook his head. "No, I'm not talking about the fact that Conner's got a drinking problem," he began.

"Oh, you mean the intervention, then?" she cut in, suddenly seeming more animated than she had this whole car ride. "Yeah, you should definitely fill them in on what happened today. You never know—Conner might stop by your house or call or something. All of our parents should know what's up so they don't just let him leave without finding out where he's going or something, you know?"

"Yeah," Andy muttered, clamping his hands tighter around the steering wheel. "I guess you're right." *And I guess this is totally pointless.* Tia was too obsessed with Conner to even think about anything else—not even the issue that had been weighing Andy down for what seemed like an eternity now. It looked like figuring out how to tell his parents that he was gay was something he'd have to do on his own.

Jessica Wakefield

Things to do for homecoming-dance committee:

— Call DJs to make sure they know what time they're supposed to show up for the interviews on Saturday.

— Double-check list of decorations for the dance — make sure we have everything and we're not over budget.

— Check with police about security for the dance. (We need to have at least one officer there all night.)

— Convince my friends that helping me with this committee will be the perfect distraction from all our love-life problems. In fact, it's been a full five minutes since I've thought about Jade and Jeremy. Ugh — I don't even like writing their names that close together!

"This one's still all soapy," Emma said, passing Jeremy back a pot big enough to fit over her head and shoulders.

Jeremy shook the excess water from his hands and turned to face his sister. The chili pot she held was covered with suds. "Hey, don't look at me," Jeremy said. "Trisha's the one doing the rinsing."

At that comment his youngest sister spun around, her brown pigtails swinging around her face. "It's not *my* fault," Trisha said. "That pot's too big. It won't fit under the faucet."

Jeremy laughed. "That's the lamest excuse I've heard all night," he teased.

"It's true," Trisha responded, her hands on her hips. "You try it."

Jeremy took the chili pot from Emma and edged over to Trisha's side of the double sink, pushing her out of the way. "The key," he said, "is moving the faucet all the way to the right and using the spray nozzle instead."

"But it's too big!" Trisha insisted, rolling her eyes. "The water will splatter everywhere."

"You mean, like this?" Jeremy aimed the nozzle straight at Trisha and gave a little squirt.

"Jeremy!" Trisha squealed, charging at him. Jeremy caught her in a solid headlock with one arm while he tickled her with his other hand. Meanwhile Emma was in hysterics on the floor.

"What's going on in here?"

Jeremy let go of Trisha and glanced at the doorway. His parents stood there watching them, his mom's arms folded over her chest.

Immediately Jeremy and his sisters straightened themselves. "Um . . . the chili pot wouldn't fit under the faucet," he explained while his sisters tried to suppress their giggles.

Mr. and Mrs. Aames exchanged doubtful smirks. "I'm impressed," Mr. Aames said, gesturing toward the puddle on the floor. "Not even done with the dishes and you've already started on the floor. Should I get you a mop?"

"Um, no, that's okay," Jeremy said. "I mean, I was going to do the floor, but then I remembered I owe Trisha a few bedtime stories."

"You never said—," Trisha started, but Emma cupped her hand over her little sister's mouth.

"I see." Mrs. Aames nodded, smiling.

Trisha wriggled free of her older sister's grasp. "Does that mean Jade is coming over again?" she asked eagerly. "She reads stories the *best*."

Jeremy felt his cheeks heat up. It was cool that his sister was so into Jade, but he didn't want her—or his parents—to get the wrong idea. He and Jade weren't serious this time, and his family shouldn't be depending on her always being around.

"No, Jade's not coming tonight," he said, squatting down to Trisha's level. "You'll have to settle for just me."

"I guess that's okay," Trisha answered. "But when is Jade coming over again?"

"Yeah," Emma jumped in. "She was cool. And when she reads to Trisha, you have a lot more time to help me with my homework."

Jeremy could feel his parents' gazes burning on his face, but he refused to meet their eyes. He knew exactly what they were thinking. *Jeremy's new girlfriend.* They would make fun of him nonstop *and* demand to meet her.

"I guess I'm not good enough on my own anymore, huh?" Jeremy joked.

"Well, she does sound like a very nice girl," Mrs. Aames piped up. He cringed. Here it came. "I look forward to meeting her."

"Is Jade your girlfriend?" Emma asked.

"Um, not exactly," he mumbled, drying his damp hands on his jeans.

"But she's a girl, and she's your friend," Trisha pointed out with her typical on-target six-year-old logic.

"Yeah," he agreed, "but—"

"Then she's your girlfriend," Emma announced.

Jeremy risked a glance over at his parents, letting out a small sigh when he saw their amused expressions. Neither of them was about to offer any help.

Oh, well, Jeremy thought. There was no sense trying to explain the complexities of boyfriend-girlfriend relationships versus casual dating to his two little sisters. Especially considering he wasn't totally solid on the topic himself.

"And then he just took off," Elizabeth finished.

Jessica swiveled back and forth on Elizabeth's desk chair, staring helplessly at her sister. Elizabeth was lying on her back on the bed, staring at the ceiling. She hadn't looked at Jessica once during the whole story she'd just told.

"Well, it sounds like you did everything you could," Jessica said, wishing that didn't sound so lame.

"I don't know," Elizabeth replied. "I keep thinking that if I had just kept my mouth shut, maybe it could have gone differently. I mean, *we're here because we love you,*" she mimicked herself. "How bad is that?"

Jessica frowned. Why was her sister always so hard on herself? "It was the truth, right?" she said. "What else were you supposed to say?"

Elizabeth propped herself up on her elbows,

finally meeting her sister's gaze. Jessica tried not to cringe at the sight of Elizabeth's red-rimmed eyes. She'd obviously been crying ever since she came home.

Jessica got up from the chair, then walked over and plopped down on the edge of Elizabeth's bed. She pushed a few strands of blond hair back behind her ears, taking a deep breath. "Lizzie," she started, using the nickname she hadn't spoken for what seemed like forever, "you can't blame yourself for what's going on with Conner. It's not your fault that he's an alcoholic, and it's *way* out of your control to stop him."

Elizabeth nodded, a small amount of light returning to her eyes. "You sound like Evan," she murmured. "He kept telling me that too."

Jessica forced a smile. "See? And he knows what he's talking about."

"I guess," Elizabeth said, sounding unconvinced. She flopped onto her back again. "He handled the intervention better than I did," she continued. "I would have really fallen apart if he hadn't been there."

"Mmmm," Jessica said, making a mental note to thank Evan for being so nice to her sister. He was really a great friend. "Yeah, Evan's a good guy," she added. "That's probably why I let myself think I was falling for him back when I was all messed up over Will and Jeremy."

19

Saying Jeremy's name out loud sent a little jab of hurt through her, and Jessica wondered if now was an okay time to bring that up. She knew her twin was going through something much heavier, but she really needed to unload. And maybe Elizabeth could use the distraction anyway.

"Um, actually," Jessica began, "I have some news about Jeremy. I didn't say anything before because I know you had to focus on the intervention, but Jeremy's back together with Jade." She hated even saying it.

"Really?" Elizabeth sounded genuinely interested, so Jessica decided it was fine to continue.

"Yeah, apparently he's over the whole catching-her-kissing-another-guy thing," she said with more than a little bitterness. "According to Jade, things have never been better between them." She pictured Jade's smug expression and how she had gloated about how blissful she and Jeremy were now.

"Wow, I'm sorry, Jess," Elizabeth said.

"I just don't get what all those guys see in her," Jessica said, tightening her hands into small fists. "Especially Jeremy. I mean, he's smart, he's nice, he's cute—why would he want to date such a manipulative little—" She stopped, realizing that Elizabeth was still staring at the ceiling, that blank, sad expression returning to her face. If she was going to distract her sister, it wasn't going to be with a tirade against Jade Wu.

20

She cleared her throat and tried again. "By the way, I volunteered to help organize the homecoming dance," she said.

"Uh-huh," Elizabeth answered.

"So I'm on the homecoming committee now," she went on, raising her voice and squirming closer to her sister to get her attention. "They still have a lot to do, and I thought it would be a good way to get my mind off . . . *other things,* if you know what I mean. Maybe you should think about—"

"Good night, girls." Jessica turned and saw their mother standing in the doorway, wearing one of her pretty flowered nightgowns. "Jess, shouldn't you get back to your room? Isn't it time you both get to sleep?" She paused, narrowing her blue eyes as she stared at Elizabeth. Jessica knew Mrs. Wakefield was just as worried about her sister as she was, but there wasn't much any of them could do. "You know," she continued softly, "often a good night's sleep will resolve issues that an entire night's worrying won't help."

"Thanks, Mom," Jessica said, figuring Elizabeth was too out of it to speak up. "Good night."

Mrs. Wakefield frowned but gave a last little wave and then disappeared down the hall.

Jessica leaned in closer to Elizabeth. "Does it ever freak you out how well she knows us?" she asked.

The faintest *almost* smile came to Elizabeth's lips. "Yeah, a little," she answered. "But we're lucky to

have that. Most parents don't know their kids at all."
She stopped, the glassy expression coming back.
"Like Conner," she said. "I mean, he basically grew
up without anyone since his mom was an alcoholic
and his dad wasn't around. That's probably why he
has all these problems now. . . ." She trailed off, and
the pain in her eyes was too much for Jessica to take.

She wished there was some way she could help,
but she knew there wasn't—just like there was no
way Elizabeth could stop Jeremy from going out
with Jade or Jade from shoving her victory in
Jessica's face.

That's why I have to focus on the dance, Jessica
told herself. And with a little more prodding, she
might even be able to get Elizabeth to help out.

"Home, sweet home," Conner muttered under
his breath as the kitchen door slammed shut behind
him. To his surprise, his mother wasn't waiting in
her usual spot at the kitchen table, and from where
he was standing, it didn't look like anyone was in the
living room either. He glanced at the clock. Eleven
forty-five. Good. He'd outlasted them all. No lec-
tures tonight.

But as he made his way through the living room
and upstairs, he could hear—or maybe feel—that his
mom and Megan were still awake. Sure enough,
when he reached the top of the stairs, he could see
light through the cracks under both of their doors.

His mother's light was dim. She probably just had the lamp next to her bed on so she could read one of her lame romance novels, but Megan's overhead light was obviously on. Conner crept closer to his sister's door and then listened closely to the noise inside. He could hear his sister's fingers tapping on her keyboard.

Homework? At midnight? He shook his head. *God, Sandy. Give it a rest.* At least it meant she wasn't a wreck from earlier, though. He'd been worrying about her the whole night as he drove around town.

With a small shrug Conner walked away and headed into his room. On the way in he stumbled over a basket of clean laundry that had been left just inside his door.

"Damn," he muttered, kicking over the basket and spilling the entire stack of folded clothes across his floor.

Great, he thought, immediately regretting his outburst. If they hadn't heard him before, they definitely knew he was home now. He waited for Megan and his mother to come running from their rooms, his chest tightening with rage at the thought of their concerned faces, but they didn't come. Megan's typing continued on the other side of the wall.

Conner picked up an armful of the rumpled laundry and threw it at his bed. Then he grabbed his pillow and flung it onto the floor. Somehow their ignoring him was making him even angrier. It was probably that whole let-him-hit-bottom-himself crap his mother had been talking about ever since she had gotten back from rehab.

When is she going to get it? Conner thought, clenching his fists so hard, the muscles in his arms and shoulders tensed too. Just because she was a drunk didn't mean that everyone else who occasionally had a drink was an alcoholic. It wasn't like Conner was showing up for school wasted or getting kicked out of country clubs every afternoon the way Mrs. Sandborn used to. So why couldn't they all just lay off?

He stalked over to his dresser and opened the top drawer, rummaging through the haphazardly stacked pairs of socks and boxers. He thought he remembered having stashed an old bottle of vodka there, but he couldn't find it.

Must have been a different drawer, he thought. In a rapid-fire process of elimination, he emptied the contents of the entire dresser, still coming up empty-handed.

Where is it? he wondered, the frustration building inside him. Then the memory clicked in place, and in two steps Conner was inside his closet, pushing aside shoes and dirty laundry. He sighed in relief when he finally spotted the nearly full bottle of vodka. Just grasping its glass neck was comforting— a precursor to the soothing warmth of the liquid sliding down his throat.

But as Conner pulled the bottle from the corner of his closet, he realized there was something stuck to the bottom of it. He peeled it off, noticing that it was a postcard. The picture was just a traditional shot of the capitol building in Sacramento, but the image triggered something in Conner—some sort of familiar feeling, though he couldn't place it.

He flipped over the postcard, his eyes going right to the message. The ink on the postcard was blurred, but he immediately recognized the handwriting. He'd received four or five of these postcards in the first year after his father left—and none since.

Disgusted, Conner threw the card on the floor and pulled the plastic-topped cork from his bottle of vodka. But as he sat down on his bed and raised the bottle to his lips, the postcard caught his eye again.

Maybe . . .

No. Conner banished the thought from his head. He'd never considered trying to find his father before, so why do it now? After all, it had been eleven years, and his dad had made a clean break—he obviously didn't want to be part of Conner's life.

But still, he couldn't help thinking that now would be a great time to pull a disappearing act of his own. He could definitely stand to get away—to a place where he wouldn't be surrounded with people psychoanalyzing his every move. And a change of scenery wouldn't hurt either. After an entire afternoon of driving down all the same old streets and seeing all the same old places, he had begun to feel like even the town was suffocating him.

Leaning forward off the bed, Conner reached for the postcard, studying the postmark as he sat on the floor. Some place called Red Bluff. He remembered looking it up when he'd first gotten the postcards as a little kid. He was pretty sure Red Bluff was about two hundred miles north—just a short, four-hour drive.

If he hasn't moved somewhere else, Conner realized. It had been a long time. How could he be sure his dad was still there?

Conner tilted the vodka to his mouth, letting the clear, odorless liquid warm his throat and soothe his nerves. Even if Mr. McDermott had left Red Bluff, it would make a good day trip—at least it would get him away from here.

He turned the bottle from side to side in his hand, watching the vodka swish inside. And if his dad *was* there? Conner knew better than to expect some tearful reunion. That wasn't what he wanted anyway. It wasn't like they had to become best buddies or anything.

Conner took another long drink. All he needed was a place to stay for a little while. And after eleven years, his father at least owed him that.

Megan Sandborn

Welcome to Ask Ally! To send Ally your question, fill out the form below:

<u>First</u> <u>name:</u> Megan <u>Last</u> <u>name:</u> Smith

<u>Gender:</u> F

<u>Age:</u> 15

<u>E-mail:</u> sandy@cal.rr.com

Please type your question below:

Okay, so . . . I'm not sure where to start. I've never written in to a site like this before, but I don't know what else to do. I think my brother's an alcoholic. That's what my mom said and all his friends. And it makes sense, with the way he's been acting.

I can hear him rummaging around in his room right now—he might even be

drinking, I don't know—and I'm
wondering if I should go talk to him
or if it's better just to leave him
alone. My mom said that we should let
him be tonight because confronting him
right now would only make things worse
(we had an intervention this
afternoon, and it didn't go so well—it
kind of just made him angrier, I
think) and that she'd deal with him
in the morning, after he had a night
to cool down, but I'm not so sure if
waiting is the best thing. Please
write back soon and tell me what to
do—I don't want him to get hurt, and
I don't want to lose him.
                 <SUBMIT QUESTION>

http://www.str8talk4teens.com/AskAlly/
                autoresponder.html
    Thanks for submitting your question
to Ask Ally. Due to the volume of e-mail
received each day, we regret that Ally
cannot answer your query personally.
But keep an eye on this site! Your
message along with a complete response
could appear in this column in the
upcoming months. And thanks for
writing! To see Ally's tip of the
day, click here.

CONNER MCDERMOTT
4:30 A.M.

Sandy—
    I wasn't going to leave a note, but I didn't want you to freak out—so don't. I'm fine. I just need to get away for a while, but I'm not going to do anything stupid. Promise.
    I'll call you.

                                    —Conner

CHAPTER
Not Serious
3

Jade strode down the sidewalk, quickening her pace to an almost jog. It was going to be tight getting in and out of House of Java during the morning rush and still making it to school on time, but it was also going to be totally worth it. Jeremy deserved a thank-you gift for giving her such a great job lead, and the fact that it would make Jessica burn with jealousy didn't hurt either.

Perfect, Jade thought as she swung open the metal-framed glass door and stepped inside. A customer was just leaving the counter, and there was only one other guy in line. Somehow she had managed to hit a slow spot in the normally nonstop flow of early morning commuters. *Just one more sign that this was a brilliant idea,* she told herself, strolling over to the counter and getting in line behind the guy waiting.

She fingered the small package in her hands, looking down at the playful dinosaur wrapping paper she'd chosen. It was just the kind of thing Jeremy would love.

31

"Can I help you?"

Jade glanced up into the eyes of her old coworker Daniel Hannigan.

"Oh, hey, Jade," he said when he saw it was her. A hint of nervousness came over his usually bored expression, and she figured he thought she was there to start a fight over being fired or something.

She smiled. "Don't worry. I'm just here to drop this off," she said, setting the box down on the counter and pushing it toward Daniel with a flirtatious smile.

Daniel's face relaxed, and he picked up the box. "For me?" he joked. "Jade, you shouldn't have."

Jade rolled her eyes, giving her straight, black hair a little shake to fluff it out. "Sorry," she said. "Maybe next time. This one's for Jeremy."

Daniel nodded. He turned the box over in his hands. "Any chance of you telling me what it is?" he asked.

Jade tilted her head, pretending to think it over. "Um . . . no," she answered with a smirk. "You'll just have to wait and watch Jeremy open it later."

Daniel shrugged, squatting down to put the gift on the ledge under the counter. "So," he said when he came back up, "you guys must be getting pretty serious if you were willing to give up an extra half hour of sleep just to surprise him."

Jade stiffened, wondering why everyone suddenly

had to use that word—*serious*. Just as she was about to argue, the small bell above the door jingled, and she turned automatically to see who had walked in. Two women in power suits and three-inch heels click-clacked their way over to the counter.

Jade quickly spun back to face Daniel. "We're *not* getting serious," she insisted, right before the women came up behind her.

Daniel gave her one of those teasing yeah-right kind of smiles, then focused his attention on the customers. "What can I get for you today?" he asked them, leaning around Jade. She frowned, then moved aside to give the women room.

Glancing at the clock, she realized that she had only fifteen minutes before homeroom. It was definitely time to go, but she couldn't help feeling this ridiculous need to stick around and make Daniel believe she was telling the truth. What was wrong with her? Since when did she care what other people thought, especially a guy she barely knew and had only worked with for, like, two seconds? *Since never,* she told herself, exhaling sharply and giving Daniel a quick wave before turning to leave.

Out on the sidewalk in the fresh air, Jade noticed that her body had completely tensed up. She jogged to her car, shaking her hands at her sides in an attempt to loosen her muscles. What was the big deal anyway? So Daniel had assumed she and Jeremy were a serious couple—what was so bad about that?

Just because Daniel—and her mom—had said it didn't mean it was true.

Sure, Jade had bought Jeremy a present, and she had gotten up extra early to deliver it—which was totally against her nature—but half the reason she had done it in the first place was because she knew how uptight Jessica would get when she saw Jeremy unwrapping the adorable, tiny stuffed dog with the little thank-you heart Jade had stuck to one of its ears. Not exactly the motive of a devoted girlfriend.

By the time Jade had reached her car, she was feeling better about Daniel's comment. He had probably just been joking anyway, but even if he wasn't, it didn't matter. Jade knew where things stood, and that's all that counted. So what if she actually enjoyed doing something nice for Jeremy? He was a nice guy, and she liked him. That's all there was to it. Daniel could believe whatever he wanted.

Elizabeth drummed her fingers against the yellow plastic surface of her desk. She'd tried to find Conner after homeroom, but he wasn't around, and she hadn't had time to find out if anyone else had seen him yet. Now she was stuck in AP history, listening to Mr. Ford's booming voice instead of being able to grill Andy, who'd slipped into class late.

Maybe he didn't show up today, she thought. The idea of him ditching school the day after the intervention made her nervous—even though it totally made sense. But this definitely wasn't a good time for Conner to be alone.

Elizabeth blinked, making an effort to concentrate on what Mr. Ford was saying—something about Russia and Stalin and Trotsky and the revolution. But all his words were blending together in her head, where one thought just repeated over and over—where was Conner right now?

I've got to get a grip, she told herself. She glanced over at Maria, who wasn't taking notes either. She was just staring straight ahead with a dazed expression.

Before leaving Conner's house yesterday, Maria had made some comment about a big fight with Ken, and Elizabeth hadn't really been able to process it in the middle of everything else. She'd figured whatever it was would blow over. But Maria and Ken hadn't looked at each other once all class. Still, it was only the morning after their blowout.

Slowly Elizabeth tore a piece of paper from her spiral-bound notebook and started scribbling.

Maria—
Are you and Ken talking yet? Is everything okay? Oh, and have you seen Conner today by any chance? Or did you happen to see if his car was in the parking lot when you came in?
—Liz

She carefully folded the note into a small square and then, when Mr. Ford turned to write on the chalkboard, tossed it across the aisle to Maria. She tapped her foot against the chair leg while she watched Maria unfold the note and read it over.

Finally Maria grabbed her pen and started writing a response. It took her a while, which made Elizabeth's heart rate shoot up.

She must know something, Elizabeth thought, barely able to restrain herself from jumping up and seizing the paper from Maria's hands. After what seemed like an eternity, Maria finished and tossed the note back.

No—haven't seen Conner or his car. Maybe he took the day off?

It's definite—Ken and I are totally over. I heard a bunch of sophomore girls talking about how much fun he was at the party last night, and I just about lost it. I can't even believe he's the same guy I was dating less than twenty-four hours ago. I mean, how could he go from being my sweet, sensitive boyfriend to Ken My-ego-won't-fit-on-this-planet Matthews overnight like that? I don't get it.

And as if it isn't bad enough that I have to listen to all the underclass girls swooning about him every time I walk down the hall, I have to sit here and stare at the back of his big, fat, swollen head for forty-five minutes every morning. Stupid seating chart.

Try not to worry too much about Conner—he'll come around, I'm sure. He knows how much you care about him.

—M

Elizabeth sighed, shutting her eyes for an instant. She knew her friend was really hurting, but somehow she just couldn't focus on Maria's problems right now. At least Ken wasn't in serious danger, and for all she knew, Conner was lying in some . . .

No, she wouldn't even let herself think it. Elizabeth glanced at the clock, surprised to find that it was actually ticking down the last minutes of class. She started stacking up all her books as quietly as possible so she could bolt at the bell.

Mr. Ford began rattling off tonight's homework assignment, but Elizabeth didn't care. She could get it from Maria later. Or maybe Andy since Maria didn't seem to be writing it down either.

When the bell rang, she was the first one out of her seat, and she ignored Mr. Ford's disapproving glare. She was out the door before the hallway had filled with students, and she immediately began surveying the area for any sign of Conner. But instead she spotted Megan, heading right for her.

Elizabeth froze, taking in the panicked expression on Megan's face along with the way her strawberry-blond bangs hung crookedly across her forehead, as if she'd been nervously running her hands through them all morning. "I tried to find you before first period," Megan said, rushing over to her. "But—you're not going to believe this." The big, dark circles under her eyes confirmed Elizabeth's fear—something had happened to Conner.

"What is it? Is he all right?" Elizabeth asked, her voice catching.

"I don't know," Megan answered. "He wasn't around when I got up this morning, but he left me this note." She held the crumpled piece of paper out to Elizabeth. "He's gone," she said.

"W-What?" Elizabeth stammered. She stared down at the note as if it were some foreign object, unable to recall how to do something as simple as read the few words written there.

"Liz, can you even believe the way Ken—" Maria stopped when she reached them. "Hey, Megan," she said. She shot Elizabeth a questioning glance. "What's wrong?"

Elizabeth gulped, glancing back down at Conner's note and finally managing to let the words make sense in her head. "Oh God," she murmured.

"I know." Megan shook her head. "How am I *not* supposed to freak out after that?" she asked.

Elizabeth took in a shaky breath, telling herself that she had to try to at least appear calm for Megan's sake. But her mind filled with image after image of Conner in horrible situations—broken down on the side of the road in the middle of nowhere, getting in a car accident, lying in a hospital where no one knew who he was or who to call.

"What did your mom say?" she asked, hoping Mrs. Sandborn had been able to give Megan the reassurance that she didn't seem capable of offering at the moment. She caught a glimpse of Tia heading toward them but kept her focus on Megan.

"She's a mess," Megan said. "She called the police as soon as I showed her the note, but they said he has to be missing for at least twenty-four hours before they can do anything. I wanted to stay with her, but she made me come to school. I guess she didn't want me to miss anything. And maybe he'll come back today, you know? While I'm here?"

Elizabeth forced a nod, even though she believed that about as much as Megan probably did.

Conner was gone—and it was entirely possible that she'd never see her boyfriend again.

Uh-oh, Andy thought, stopping suddenly as he rounded the corner. Elizabeth, Megan, Tia, and Maria were gathered in a close circle. It could mean only one thing. *Conner crisis.*

He adjusted his backpack on his shoulder and slowly walked over to them. No one seemed to realize that he was there, so instead of interrupting to ask what was up, Andy just listened.

"Do you have *any* ideas, Tia?" Megan pleaded, her voice cracking as if she were on the verge of tears, or on the verge of pulling out her hair, or—definitely on the verge of something. He wondered if anyone else had noticed that her blue shirt was buttoned wrong.

Tia shook her head, then bit her bottom lip. "Normally I'd say he probably just went over to Seth's or the beach or something to chill out, but I can't really see Conner leaving a note if he wasn't—" She stopped, shooting a nervous glance at Megan. "Well, if he wasn't going farther away."

"I just wish we knew where he was—or when he was coming back," Maria said.

Andy cleared his throat, and they all turned in his direction. "Hey," he said. "I'm guessing Conner took off?"

Megan nodded. "Do you have any ideas where he would have gone?" she asked.

Andy frowned, wishing he could come up with something to calm her down. Megan was a great girl—he didn't like seeing her so wrecked. "No. I didn't even know he was gone until I heard you guys talking about it." What a shocker—Andy being the last one to know something. He hadn't been clued in to Conner's drinking problem until right before the intervention. "What was in the note?" he asked, running a hand through his curly red hair.

"Not much," Megan said with a sigh. "Just that he needed a break and I shouldn't worry."

Typical Conner, Andy thought. Yeah, the guy had major stuff going on, but couldn't he think about someone besides himself for just once? His sister was obviously torn up over this, and . . . well, Andy wasn't really in the best place to deal with one of his best friends pulling a disappearing act either. Conner knew what was going on with him too. He'd barely reacted when Andy told him he was gay, but Andy had figured the guy needed some time to let it all sink in. Instead he bolted without ever thinking that Andy could really need him.

"Jerk," Andy couldn't help muttering.

"What?" Tia's mouth fell open, and she looked at him like he'd just insulted the pope.

Andy let out his breath, realizing he shouldn't have let that one escape. "It's just—he knows we're all going to worry," he said. "But I'm sure he's telling the truth. All he needs is a break, you know? Maybe it's not such a big deal."

Elizabeth gave him an even harsher look than the one Tia had flashed him, as if he had just suggested they all go out and kick puppies for fun.

"Not a big deal?" she echoed, her blue-green eyes full of confusion. "How could you even say that?"

"Seriously," Tia chimed in. "I don't think you would if you'd seen the mood he was in when he left his house yesterday after the intervention."

Great, Andy thought. Now they were all going to lecture him on his insensitivity until he acknowledged that Conner was in big trouble and joined in with all the fingernail biting and what-do-we-do-now talk.

"That's not what I meant," he said. It wasn't that

he didn't care about Conner—why else would he have showed up for the intervention? Andy knew Conner was going through something huge, but he couldn't help wondering when someone else would realize that Conner wasn't the only one.

"It's okay, Andy," Megan said. "I know we all just want Conner to be okay."

Andy gave her a half smile of appreciation and nodded along with the rest of the group.

"Yeah," he said, looking at Megan's tired, tense face. "Hey—Conner's always been pretty self-reliant," he reminded her. "He can take care of himself, at least long enough to get himself back home where we can help."

The bell rang, and everyone around them started rushing off to second-period classes.

"We'll talk later," Tia said before they all headed in different directions.

Andy was almost relieved to walk away on his own. He shuffled down the hall at a casual pace, not too worried about being late for calculus. He could probably just slip in the back door anyway—or skip class altogether. Who was going to notice? He wasn't one of those Conner types, where the universe revolved around his every move. He was more like some distant planet in the solar system—Pluto, maybe. No one spent much time wondering what was going on there, right?

Maria Slater

Sociology 101
Mr. King

Define the following terms and give an example of each.

Social Control

Definition: the way a group makes sure its members conform to its norms, values, and ideology

Example: If, say, a quarterback on a football team didn't hang out with the rest of his teammates and do all the same moronic things they did—like consume five cases of beer after every win, go to all the parties, and participate in various dumb chants (like "drink, drink, drink!"), they'd probably give him a hard time and start calling him a wuss in front of all the freshman girls who were supposed to idolize him. And if he had a girlfriend with a brain that he occasionally put ahead of football, they would probably start calling him "whipped" and harass him until he either joined the crowd or quit the team.

Status

   Definition: the specific position a person occupies in a group
   Example: On a football team, for example, a person could be a benchwarmer, which is kind of a low-status position, or he could be the star quarterback, which—at least at SVH—would make him roughly equivalent to a god.

Role

   Definition: how a person in a particular position is supposed to act
   Example: When a football player is just a benchwarmer, no one cares what he does or who he dates, and he can be a pretty sweet guy. But

once he becomes Mr. Macho, King of High-school Football, everyone—including him—decides he needs to act like a newly thawed Neanderthal with only two functioning brain cells—one for drinking beer and the other for calling plays.

Role Conflict

Definition: what happens when a person holds two or more roles that are incompatible

Example: It would be impossible for someone to be both a decent boyfriend (the first role) and a star quarterback (the second role), so a guy would have to choose to either act normally and keep his ego in the room or start going to all the jock parties, acting like a complete jerk, and letting his ego blow up roughly to the size of Texas. Apparently it's an easy choice for some people.

Andy Marsden

I'm ready to admit it—I, Andy Marsden, have actually watched made-for-TV movies about gay teenagers. And I've learned that there's some basic stuff that always happens in every one. Like, there's always this huge buildup before the main character "comes out." And then, after he does it, all the other characters have these way-over-the-top reactions. They either start avoiding him because they're totally unable to deal with it or they instantly try to hook him up with their favorite gay hairdresser or something. And then, of course, they end up accepting it and helping the guy deal.

Yes, I get that TV (especially _bad_ TV) isn't real life. But I guess I still thought that telling my friends I was gay would cause some kind of effect. Instead they're acting like I'm just some minor character in everything going on around us. But if I'm the one with the "issue" or whatever, shouldn't I have more than a bit part?

CHAPTER 4
A Day Without Crying

Jade grinned the second she spotted Jessica Wakefield alone by her locker. It looked like Jessica was already having a less than ideal morning. She was wearing a pair of faded jeans with a plain gray T-shirt—not her usual style—and strands of her light blond hair were coming out of her messy ponytail.

"Great," Jessica muttered as she tried to stuff a few more books into her crammed locker.

"Don't you just hate these puny lockers?" Jade asked, coming up behind her.

Jessica started, then whirled around to face Jade. She frowned. "Don't you have a class to get to or something?" she said.

Jade smiled. "Just study hall," she replied. "No need to hurry." She leaned on the locker next to Jessica's, enjoying the sight of her one-time friend so off balance. The girl had *almost* ruined things between Jade and Jeremy, and then—as if that weren't enough—she'd gotten her fired from House of Java. But now Jade was the one back on top, and Jessica was clearly not loving life right now.

"So, Jess," Jade began in an overly warm tone, as if she and Jessica were best friends, "I heard you're on the homecoming committee now. Does that mean I'll see you at the dance?"

Jessica's jaw tightened. "I guess," she said, keeping her gaze focused on her locker as she tried to reorganize the contents to make room for the extra books.

"That's great," Jade said. "Maybe we could all hang out together. You know, me and Jeremy, and you and your—" She stopped, pretending to have caught herself. "Oh, wait, you probably don't *have* a date, right?"

Jessica's eyes narrowed into tiny slits.

"Oops—sorry," Jade said, widening her own eyes in mock innocence. "Well, don't worry about it—I'm sure you'll find *someone* to go with. Maybe Josh Radinsky? After all, I'm done with him now."

In one swift motion Jessica slammed her locker shut. "I'm sorry," she answered, shaking her head, "*who* did you say you were going with?"

Jade grinned, thrilled to have the chance to rub it in Jessica's face again. "Jeremy, of course. We've gotten really close over the—"

"*Just* Jeremy?" Jessica asked, raising her eyebrows. "I thought you preferred to date two or three at a time."

Jade felt her chest tighten, and from the burn on her cheeks she knew her face must be getting red. "For your information, Jeremy is more than enough," she snapped. How was it that Jessica always found a way to get to her?

"Oh, please," Jessica said. "As if you even care about him."

"Of course I care about him!" Jade blurted out, the strength of her words catching her off guard. She forced herself to take a cleansing breath—her mom's term for the way she calmed herself down when she felt like hitting one of her snotty customers at the bank where she worked as a teller. Then Jade spun around and headed down the hallway, fuming.

Okay, so I care, she told herself. *I care about Jeremy.* But that was fine. It wasn't like she was Jeremy's love-struck girlfriend and she was going to start waiting by the phone for him to call or anything.

She stormed into her study-hall classroom, catching the attention of a few freshman girls who were clustered around one of the smaller rectangular tables. Jade sent them a harsh glare, and they all looked back down at their notebooks immediately. She walked over to a quiet study cube in the back corner and dropped her books on the desk with a thud.

There's no reason to freak out here, Jade told herself. Especially when what had upset her so much in the first place was that Jessica had been able to fluster her—just when she was really starting to enjoy watching the girl squirm.

Jade settled into the hard plastic chair and opened up her history textbook. Sure, she cared about Jeremy. But she wasn't *attached*. Because that simply wasn't possible. She didn't let herself get attached—to anyone.

"I just can't belicve it," Tia stage-whispered, practically twirling her long, brown hair into knots. She leaned forward, resting her elbows on the square table that she, Andy, and Maria were sharing. "I mean, he's gone—*él partió, él es ido, él ha desaparecido*—"

"I think we get the point, Tia," Andy interrupted.

"Sorry," Tia said. "When I get stressed, I start talking like my mother. I just can't believe Conner really left."

"Yeah, I know," Andy muttered. The low hum of individual voices around them was blending into one droning buzz. But Tia's constant chatter managed to rise above the rest of the noise, and right now Andy felt like it was making his skull vibrate.

"Where's Liz anyway?" he said, glancing at the open door, half expecting to see her walk in with a pink slip excusing her tardiness. Elizabeth never got to class late without an excuse from one teacher or another. He'd been counting on her help with some of the really tough calculus problems he had for homework. She was one of those superbrains who was actually good at English *and* math. He still wasn't convinced the girl was all human.

"She's taking a makeup exam for Ms. Dalton," Maria explained.

"Great," Andy said, flinging down his pencil. "What am I supposed to do now? Figure this stuff out on my own?"

Maria gave him a funny look. "Are you okay, Andy? You seem a little tense."

Andy glanced at Maria in surprise. Wait—was one of his friends actually noticing him? There must be some kind of blip in the space-time continuum.

"Yeah, I'm okay," he said, letting his shoulders slump forward. "It's just that—well, you know, I've had a lot going on lately, and—"

"Tell me about it," Tia interrupted. "All this stuff with Conner is really making us all crazy."

Andy held back a groan. If she had just let him finish, then she—and Maria—would know that for once he was *not* talking about Conner McDermott. He needed someone to tell him how he should give his parents the biggest shock of their lives, and he kept hoping that one of his friends would rise to the occasion.

It's not worth it, he decided. Why bother trying to ask his friends for advice when they wouldn't even let him get out a complete sentence?

"I'm not that close to him," Maria said, "but still, to have one of your friends be an alcoholic—" She

51

put her hand on Andy's back. "It must be really hard for you—and you too, Tia," she added, looking across the table.

"We've known Conner since we were little kids," Tia said. "And I just don't get how things could have gotten so bad. I mean, I know he's had it rough, but he always seemed to have everything so under control—until now."

Andy cringed. It was all he could do to keep himself from knocking Maria's arm off his back, and if he'd had a spare sock, he would have stuffed it in Tia's mouth ten minutes ago.

"Are you sure you don't have any idea where he could be, Andy?" Tia asked. It was more than he could take. They'd been over this five hundred times in the last two hours.

"No," he answered flatly. "And look, I don't mean to be rude or anything, but I really don't feel like talking about Conner anymore, okay?" Maria stiffened in her chair, and Andy could feel her and Tia exchanging a what's-up-with-him? look across the table. He didn't know how Maria could be so oblivious—he'd told her earlier that week how sick he was of everyone ignoring his problems.

Shaking his head, he picked up his pencil and pretended to start solving an equation in his notebook, even though he had no clue what he was doing without Elizabeth's help.

"I'm sorry, Andy," Maria said. "I know you've had

a lot on your mind recently, and watching Conner lose it must be sending you over the edge."

Andy bit his lip to keep from laughing. She was *still* talking about Conner. Had *he* been speaking a foreign language this time?

"We don't need to get into it, but if you need . . ." Maria trailed off, and he looked up, curious. Her gaze was locked on something just outside the classroom door. Andy followed her line of vision to see Ken in the hallway, talking to Becky Stevens—a girl from El Carro who flirted with anyone in a football uniform. She was obviously one of Ken's newest groupies. And Ken didn't seem too bugged by it—he had a big, dopey grin on his face.

"Don't look, Maria," Tia instructed. "What a jerk—what is it about football that turns guys into total morons? Not that Angel was ever that way, but still—"

"There must be a full moon or something," Maria cut in, her voice empty. "This has just been a terrible week."

"Tell me about it," Tia agreed. "Between Conner and Ken . . ."

That was it. Andy dropped his head to the table and closed his eyes while Maria and Tia babbled on about the various problems with the men in their lives—excluding him, of course. Obviously they had both totally forgotten that he had come out to them barely two weeks ago. Or maybe they had misunderstood and thought that when he said he was gay, he just meant he was really happy. Whatever.

One thing had become abundantly clear to Andy in the last twenty-four hours. More than anything, he needed to focus on himself—for once. And none of his friends seemed capable of helping him out with that.

"Where is everyone?" Elizabeth asked, scanning the cafeteria for the rest of her friends.

"I saw Jessica in the hall," Evan said, picking a french fry off Elizabeth's tray. "She said something about a homecoming meeting, I think."

"Oh, right," Elizabeth said. She could vaguely remember her sister babbling about the homecoming-dance committee on the car ride to school this morning. "And Maria's eating in the *Oracle* office so she doesn't have to deal with Ken."

As if on cue, a roar went up from the table where all the football players were sitting. She glanced over to see what the excitement was.

"Oh, good," she said flatly. "Josh Radinsky set a new record for stuffing grapes in his mouth."

Evan chuckled. "One small step for Josh, one giant step for Sweet Valley High," he joked. He shook his head. "So what about Tia and Andy?" he asked. "Any idea on their location?"

"Maybe they're eating outside or something,"

Elizabeth replied. Honestly, she didn't mind that they weren't around. She wasn't really up for another intense powwow about Conner since she knew they wouldn't get anywhere anyway.

Evan grabbed a couple more fries. "You don't mind, do you?" he asked.

She narrowed her eyes, trying to focus on his question. "What? Oh—no, take as many as you want."

Evan grinned and took a handful of the french fries, then dropped them onto his tray. "I'll get you more if you run out," he said. "I just don't like to buy them for myself."

Elizabeth looked over at the salad and veggie sandwich on his tray. *Right. Health nut.*

"I read somewhere that fried food is actually good for you as long as it comes off someone else's tray," he continued, his bright blue eyes gleaming.

She knew she should give him some kind of polite smile, but she just couldn't manage it.

"Um, that was my poor attempt at a joke, in case you weren't sure," Evan said. He paused, shifting in his seat when she didn't respond. "You really should eat something," he added, pointing at her untouched turkey sandwich. "Food's important, especially for someone in your shape."

Elizabeth started. "What shape?" she asked, sitting up straighter. She'd thought she was doing a good job of seeming okay. So far she'd made it through the day without crying once—which felt like a pretty major achievement.

Evan leaned closer to her, pushing his tray out of the way. "No offense, but you look bad," he said, his tone serious. "I mean, you *look* great—as usual—but you're, I don't know, it's like you're not even here."

Elizabeth glanced up to meet his gaze, feeling strange about the way he stared back without blinking.

"Look, you don't have to fake it with me, okay, Liz? I was there. I saw Conner run out—I know how much that has to hurt."

Elizabeth gulped, letting her shoulders sag back down. Somehow she didn't feel the need to prove anything to him or *be* anything she wasn't. It would be so nice to just let everything pour out . . . all the thoughts that had been racing through her brain since yesterday. She'd said some of it to Jessica, but Jessica didn't know Conner the way Evan did. Maria was a mess over Ken, Tia was wound so tight, she seemed ready to explode, and Andy had totally clammed up.

Taking a deep breath, she broke eye contact with Evan and looked down at her tray, clasping her hands tightly around her soda.

"The truth?" she almost whispered. "I can't help feeling responsible. For all of this, not just the inter-vention. I mean, I should have noticed the signs that something wasn't right a long time ago. Tia told me

56

straight out that she thought he had a drinking problem, and I ignored her." She stopped, wondering what Evan would say if he knew the rest, the part she couldn't bring herself to admit. "I was so selfish," she said. The tears she'd held back all day started to collect behind her eyelids, and she blinked them back.

Evan reached out and covered her hand with his. "Liz, you are the least selfish person I know," he said firmly. "Yeah, there was some messed-up stuff going on with you and Conner and Tia, but this is totally separate. It's not easy for anyone to spot a drinking problem—especially with someone like Conner. He's not exactly big on sharing his feelings, you know? In fact, he's so good at hiding them that it's hard to even tell what kind of mood he's in most of the time."

Elizabeth nodded, afraid to trust herself to speak. There was no way she was going to lose it here, in the cafeteria in front of all their classmates. "You don't understand," she finally said. "It's not just that I *couldn't* see there was something wrong with Conner—it's that I didn't *want* to."

"Of course you didn't want to," he argued. "No one wants to believe that—"

"That's not what I mean," she interrupted, getting frustrated. Even though his hand on hers was comforting, it wasn't right somehow, and she pulled away. "It wasn't that I wanted to believe he was okay," she explained. "It was more like I just wanted

Tia to be wrong. I think I knew deep down that Conner was in trouble, but I didn't listen to Tia because I didn't want to admit that she knows Conner better than I do." The words spilled out before she could stop them, and she looked down at the table, wondering what Evan must be thinking of her.

"That's why I'm a pathetic girlfriend," she added, tightening her grip on the soda. "I probably could have helped him if I hadn't turned his problems into some kind of *contest* between me and Tia. Or even if I couldn't have helped, I could have at least backed off. It was probably all the pressure I was putting on him that made him start drinking in the first place."

"Liz, that is so wrong," Evan blurted out. "It's never your fault that someone you care about is an alcoholic," he went on. "You have to get that it's not you. There wasn't anything you could have done or *not* done. And besides, this is Conner. As in the most bullheaded, stubborn guy I've ever known. If you *had* realized earlier on that he had a problem—or admitted it to yourself, or believed Tia, or whatever—I can tell you exactly what would have happened. He would have shut you out. I'm not trying to say Conner doesn't care about you or that your opinion doesn't mean a lot to him—because I know it does," he added quickly. "But you know just as well as I do that Conner doesn't like to listen to people telling him he's wrong—no matter who it is. Not even Megan could have gotten through to him, and I think you know how much she means to him."

Elizabeth bit her lip, caught off guard by the intensity of his words. He obviously really believed it. He didn't blame her, even after she'd told him what she'd been afraid to say to anyone. And he made sense too—Conner had shut Megan out, and Elizabeth knew for a fact that she was the most important person in his life.

"Look at Conner's mom," Evan continued. "She's a perfect example. She never would have stopped if a judge hadn't *sentenced* her to rehab. And she had plenty of people telling her she had a problem, including Conner, her own son."

Elizabeth nodded slowly. Even though Jessica, her mom, and everyone else had been telling her that none of this was her fault, somehow she hadn't been able to buy it. But Evan was so clear and *persuasive*. And he knew Conner better than her family did, so she felt like she could trust him somehow.

"Thanks," she said. "That—it actually helps."

"No problem," Evan said with a shrug. "Anytime," he added, popping another french fry in his mouth.

She had a feeling that with Evan, that wasn't just something he said. He really meant it—and she was starting to realize she should be pretty grateful for that.

Ken Matthews

Thursday:

2:45 P.M.—Football practice

5:00 P.M.—Pizza with the team

Friday:

6:00 A.M.—Sprints with running backs before school

Lunch—in Coach Riley's office to review plays for weekend game

2:30 P.M.—football practice

7:00 P.M.—pregame get-together at Bruce's; carbo load

Saturday:

10:00 A.M.—pregame rally at SVH field

1:00 P.M.—game time

6:00 P.M.—meet up with guys; party at Todd Wilkins's house

Sunday:

11:00 A.M.—Review game tapes with Coach; help prepare new drill for Monday's practice

Rest!

Wow. A couple of good plays and suddenly I have to start making lists for my time again. At least with all this stuff going on, I won't be sitting around thinking about Maria nonstop. Right. As if I can get my mind off her anyway.

I just don't see why she couldn't get how important it was to me to finally have my old life back. What did she expect? That I wouldn't jump at being able to play on the team again, in my old position? Was it just some twisted thing where she only liked me when I was down?

I mean, it's not like I don't care about her anymore—I do. Of course I do. But I can't turn down the chance to play football, hang out with all my old friends, and maybe even get a college scholarship. This time I'm not letting it all slip away from me. And if that's the only way she wants me . . . then I guess maybe she's the one who didn't ever really care.

Everything's Changed

Andy ticked off his useless friends on his fingers as he made his way through the student parking lot to his car. Trying to talk to Tia was pointless—she couldn't concentrate on anything but Conner. Trying to talk to Maria was even worse. She was so messed up over her breakup with Ken that she could barely keep up with Tia's misery over Conner. Trying to talk to Conner was impossible—he was gone. So maybe he should just flip a coin. Heads, he'd spill the news to his parents tonight. Tails, he'd drive across the border and hide in Mexico until he was, oh, about forty-five?

He sighed, wishing the options didn't seem equally intimidating. Finally he reached his old Cadillac and jammed his key in the lock. Swinging open the heavy door, he threw his backpack onto the passenger side. He was about to slide into his seat when he heard familiar voices nearby.

Glancing up, he saw Elizabeth and Evan headed over to Elizabeth's Jeep. Suddenly he realized that he had two more friends he hadn't even tried talking to.

In fact, when he'd called Evan to let him know what was going on with him, Evan had been totally cool about it. He'd even offered to talk whenever Andy wanted.

That would definitely be now, Andy thought, shutting his door and making his way over.

"Hey, guys," he greeted them.

"Andy," Evan said, clapping him on the back. "What's up? How've you been?"

"Oh, you know, okay, I guess," Andy said. "I mean, with Conner and everything," he added, figuring that's what Evan meant since it seemed to be the only thing on everyone's minds. "But there is something I wanted to talk to you guys about . . . if you have a minute."

"Yeah, of course," Elizabeth said, tilting her head in concern.

Andy swallowed hard. This was it—he actually had an audience. Now, if he could just get the words out. "Well, I . . . do you remember when—"

"I know what you're going to say, Andy," Elizabeth interrupted, reaching up to rub her forehead. "I'm sorry I snapped at you this morning. I was really stressed out when Megan first told me he was gone, but I shouldn't have taken it out on you."

Andy's mouth hung open as he tried to process what she was saying. He couldn't even—oh, wait, he did know what she meant. In the hallway earlier she'd been upset at something he'd said. "Um, thanks," he managed, forcing a weak smile so Elizabeth would know he wasn't angry. "But actually, that's not what I wanted to talk about," he said, trying to regain his previous train of thought.

Elizabeth frowned. "What is it, Andy?" she asked. "You look nervous."

He laughed. Now there was an understatement. He didn't even know why it was still scary to bring this up. Maybe because it seemed like everyone had forgotten his big admission, so it was almost like "coming out" or whatever all over again. "So—what I told you guys," he began. "About what I realized."

"Wait—you know we're all okay with that, right?" Elizabeth cut in. "I mean, maybe we haven't talked about it much with everything else going on, but of course it doesn't matter to us."

"Absolutely, man," Evan chimed in, nodding vigorously. "As far as I'm concerned, nothing's changed. You're still the same guy you always were." Elizabeth and Evan exchanged smiles as though congratulating themselves for their liberal views. *What do you mean, "nothing's changed"?* Andy thought. Everything had changed for him—why couldn't anyone understand that?

"But—"

"No buts," Evan insisted. "Don't spend another second thinking about it. We're all still here for you."
Really? Where?

"And besides, you don't need anything else

weighing on your mind right now. Dealing with Conner is more than enough," Elizabeth added.

"You can say that again," Andy muttered, but he knew they weren't getting the sarcasm. This was truly ridiculous. "Well, thanks," he said awkwardly. "I guess I'll see you tomorrow." He turned to walk back to his car.

"Catch you later," Evan called after him. Andy jerked one hand into the air without turning around.

What's the deal? Andy wondered, plunking himself into the driver's seat of his car. Why couldn't any of his friends ever take him seriously? He was sick of being their comic relief. Happy-go-lucky, always-ready-to-make-a-joke Andy. That was how his friends seemed to view him. *Although now I'm happy-go-lucky, always-ready-to-make-a-joke* gay *Andy,* he thought.

Somehow it didn't seem to be much of a distinction.

"That was a tough practice," Stan Ramsey complained as he emerged from the shower room, a white towel wrapped around his waist. Jeremy watched as Stan walked past the first bench, where a few other players were getting dressed and stuffing things into duffel bags, and joined him and Trent Maynor in the back.

"Seriously," Trent agreed. "What got into Coach today anyway? I mean, it's not like we messed up our last game or anything, so he can't be punishing us. Any clue, Aames?"

Jeremy slipped a white cotton T-shirt over his head. "Hello? How long have you guys been on this team anyway—four years, right?"

Trent and Stan nodded, staring at him blankly.

Jeremy rolled his eyes. "We have a bye this weekend—no game. Coach always runs us ragged when he knows we have the weekend to recover." He craned his neck to see over his friend's shoulder and waved to a few teammates who were heading out.

As captain, Jeremy was always the last one to leave at the end of practice. And Trent and Stan usually hung around with him, rehashing practice or other stuff going on.

"Yeah, I forgot we were off this weekend," Trent said, stretching his arms out over his head.

"So, since we *are* off," Stan said, reaching into his locker for his clothes, "what are you guys going to do? Are you going to Katie's party tomorrow night?"

"Yeah—it's supposed to be huge," Trent replied. "I was planning on skipping it, but since we don't have a game . . ." He shrugged, looking at Jeremy. "Are you going?" he asked.

"I was thinking I would," Jeremy said. He'd been kind of psyched for the chance to totally unwind and have fun, no pressure. Lately his social life had been a little too stressful, and he was definitely ready for a change of pace. "You guys want to head over together?" he suggested as he yanked on his socks.

"Well . . . I sort of told Linda I'd go with her," Stan said reluctantly, adjusting his belt buckle.

Jeremy laughed, exchanging an amused glance with Trent. Stan had been hung up on Linda for pretty much forever, and now that they'd finally hooked up Stan didn't make a move without checking with Linda first.

"So, we can all go together," Jeremy said. He stood up and slammed his locker shut. "We can drag Stephanie along too," he added, referring to another of their good friends. "And I was thinking I'd invite Jade."

"What?" Trent whipped around, giving Jeremy one of his piercing looks, his dark eyes practically shooting off sparks. "After what she pulled on you— you're still seeing that girl?"

Jeremy sank back down on the bench. "Yeah, I am," he said. "But it's different this time, really."

"And the difference is . . . ," Trent prodded.

"I'll tell you what the difference is," Stan said, leaning over to zip his gym bag closed. "Jeremy thinks Jade is hot, so he doesn't care if she kissed that Sweet Valley guy."

"Oh, man, I hope that's not it," Trent said before Jeremy could respond. He clapped a hand on Jeremy's shoulder. "Haven't you learned yet? First Jessica lied to you, then Tia totally played me while she was still with her boyfriend, and Jade cheated on you. It's time to forget about SVH girls."

Jeremy sighed. He'd been worried his friends would give him a hard time over this.

"The point is, she's already burned you once. Why are you going back for more?" Stan asked.

"Oh, are you guys worried I'm going to get hurt?" Jeremy teased in an exaggerated baby-talk voice. "That's so sweeeet."

Stan tossed his towel at Jeremy's face, but he caught it midair and threw it into the basket over by the showers.

"Okay," Jeremy relented, shaking his head. "I appreciate the two of you looking out for me, but I've got things under control."

"We just don't want to see you get your heart trampled again," Stan said with a shrug. "You *are* the sensitive one, you know," he joked.

"Yeah, whatever," Jeremy said. "But you don't need to worry about me. I get it—Jade's fun, but she's not the kind of girl you get into a serious relationship with. And that's *fine*. Why shouldn't I have a good time with a cool girl if that's all either of us wants?"

He turned and slung his bag over his shoulder, ready for this conversation to be over. He didn't mind the fact that his friends cared about him, but he was sick of talking about relationships, or nonrelationships, or whatever. He was done with all that—moving on. And it felt really good.

*   *   *

I can do this, Jade told herself, smoothing down the long, conservative black skirt she'd changed into after cheerleading practice. She'd never had trouble getting a job before because she always made a great first impression, but after losing her last two jobs, she couldn't help thinking about how important this one was. And the extra pressure wasn't helping.

Jade slipped three quarters into the parking meter next to her black Nissan, took a deep breath, and strode down the sidewalk. She'd managed to get a parking spot only a block away from the sushi bar Jeremy had told her about—a perfect distance for the fresh air to calm her mind without the wind messing up her hair.

If she didn't get a job—and keep it this time— her father would stop sending child-support checks. Again. Even though he was required to pay by law, Mr. Wu refused to send money unless Jade was "pulling her own weight," as he liked to put it. And as much as Jade and her mom needed the money, Jade knew her mother didn't have the energy or the resources to fight her ex-husband in court again. It had been hard enough the first time around.

I can do this, she repeated in her head as she walked by coffeehouses, boutiques, and art galleries. The sidewalks seemed especially crowded, as if the entire city of Sweet Valley had been let off work early for some reason.

Why aren't they all sitting behind desks somewhere?

she wondered as she maneuvered around three women in tailored suits and a man in business casual—pressed shirt, jacket, khakis, shiny shoes, no tie. And why did they all seem to be directly in front of her and moving at the speed of snails? Jade felt her shoulders tensing and knew she needed to calm down. If only cheerleading hadn't been so miserable. Jessica had totally avoided her, and even Tia had ignored her, probably out of some kind of twisted loyalty to Jessica. Meanwhile Melissa and her crew were still being cold to her over that stupid little fling with Josh Radinsky, who apparently *belonged* to Lila Fowler or something stupid like that.

But so what if the whole squad hated her? Jade had better things to do than hang around those losers anyway—like spend time with Jeremy.

A smile crept over her face as she thought about him. He really did seem to be the only positive thing in her life. Somehow just picturing his face calmed and excited her all at once—and just in time. Two shops down, Jade could see the sign for the sushi bar.

She stopped outside, examining the old brick building. It had large picture windows and a tall, oak door. The sign sticking out above the door said Kitayama in white script on a black background, and tacked below it was a second sign, reading Open for Business Soon!

Jade reached up to smooth down her hair, then stepped inside, surveying the interior. Instead of regular dining tables there were low benches sur-rounded by pillows—*kotatsu* tables, Jade thought she remembered hearing them called once. Obviously working here would be slightly different from serving nachos and beer at First and Ten.

"Can I help you?"

The deep voice startled her, but she managed not to flinch. Instead she turned around with a wide smile pasted on her lips. "Yes. My name is Jade Wu," she said, extending her arm to the man standing there. "My friend Jeremy Aames told me you might be hiring new waitresses or hostesses. I'd like to apply."

The man squinted thoughtfully as he shook her hand, then smiled. "Greg Johnson," he introduced himself. That was the man Jeremy had mentioned, but Jeremy had left out the fact that he was only about thirty years old and attractive, in an outdoorsy way. He wasn't Japanese either, but Jeremy had told her that. Apparently the guy had spent a lot of time in Japan and fell in love with the culture, so he wanted to replicate it here. "So Mr. Aames sent you our way?" he said.

Jade shifted nervously. "Actually his son, Jeremy—not Mr. Aames himself," she replied.

Mr. Johnson laughed. "I was referring to Jeremy," he said.

"Oh," Jade said, biting her lip. How was she sup-posed to know that? Jeremy was only seventeen, hardly a *Mister*. She forced a laugh that, to her, sounded totally fake, but hopefully Mr. Johnson hadn't picked up on it. He was still smiling down at her, which seemed like a good sign, but Jade couldn't tell if he was simply amused or if he thought she was a complete idiot.

"Why don't you take a seat and I'll ask you a few questions?" he suggested.

"Sure. At the *kotatsu* table?" Jade asked, careful with her pronunciation.

Mr. Johnson's eyebrows shot up. "Uh, no, at the bar," he said, leading her to the rear of the room. Jade followed him tentatively, noticing his hiking boots and canvas pants. He looked like he'd come straight from scaling a rock face somewhere.

"So," he began once they had settled onto a couple of stools, "have you worked in a Japanese restaurant before?"

"No," she answered, "but I've been to Japan. I was only six, but I remember bits and pieces." She'd gone with her dad on one of his many business trips. It was actually one of the few good memories she had of when her parents were together.

"Well, have you done any waitressing before?" Mr. Johnson asked.

Here was the sticky part. "Yes, I have," she answered smoothly. "I worked at the Zephyr Grille during the summer after my sophomore year and for part of junior year, and then I, um, worked at First and Ten."

Just don't ask why I left, she begged silently.

"Well, that's enough for me," Mr. Johnson said, waving one hand in the air. He got up and walked around to the back side of the bar. Jade stiffened, uncertain how to react. Did that mean she had the job? How could he decide so quickly?

"I'm sorry," Jade said, searching his face for some explanation. "Did I . . . miss something?"

Mr. Johnson chuckled, and Jade tried to smile, but she wasn't sure what was going on.

"No, no," he said with a smile. "You're fine. But I don't do the hiring. I leave that to my partner. He'll want to do an official interview." He pulled a notebook from underneath the bar and opened it on the counter, tapping the paper with his pen. "Hmmm. It doesn't look like he has a lot of open appointments," he said, scanning the pages and flipping forward. "Is nine o'clock Sunday morning okay?"

Ugh—that was like before dawn, wasn't it? But she couldn't exactly say that to a potential future boss.

"It's fine," she chirped.

"Good," Mr. Johnson said. "If Jackie likes you, you'll have a job. How's that sound?"

Jade restrained herself from letting out a relieved sigh. "That sounds great," she said. "Thank you."

"Just write your phone number down for me so Jackie can call if he needs to reschedule," Mr. Johnson said, handing Jade his pen along with a scrap of paper.

She scribbled down her information, then gave him back the pen and paper. The corners of her mouth were beginning to feel stretched out from all the smiling.

"It was nice to meet you," she said, holding out her hand for another firm handshake.

As soon as she was back on the street, Jade practically floated back to her car. She had a feeling that if Mr. Johnson liked her, she was in. Soon enough she'd have a job again, a solid paycheck.

And it was all thanks to Jeremy. The little stuffed dog wasn't enough—she needed to do something more. *Like stop by for a little surprise visit,* she decided. After she'd finished her mom's errands, maybe she could pop by Jeremy's house just to let him know in person how much she appreciated his help. That would definitely make this day perfect.

Conner McDermott

San Mateo. San Francisco. Vallejo. Woodland. Colusa. Orland. Corning.

I've been on the road for hours since I left home early this morning—minus breaks for food and walking around—and I'm finally just thirty miles out of Red Bluff. Thirty miles away from my dad—if he's there.

I'm a little worried that all I can get on the radio now is country music.

Welcome to Red Bluff

"Elizabeth!" Terri snapped.

Elizabeth cringed at the sound of her boss's shrill voice. Was she really about to be yelled at for the millionth time tonight?

"Yes?" she answered. She looked up from the glass top of the makeup counter she had been washing and stared right into Terri's beady, angry eyes. Terri held a tube of creamy pink lipstick in her inch-long, bright red nails. "Can you tell me what season this color is from?" she demanded.

"Um, spring," Elizabeth guessed. "No, wait," she said quickly, observing the way Terri's frown had deepened. "Summer."

"Very good," Terri said, a saccharine smile stretching across her thin lips. "Now," she began, "do you mind telling me why you just stocked our entire fall display with summer tones?"

Elizabeth felt an enormous lump in her throat. "Did I?" she asked. "I'm sorry, Terri. I don't know what's wrong with me tonight," she lied. So far she had dumped a tray of eye-shadow samples on the floor, broken a bottle of the most expensive perfume they carried, and spilled a jar of nail polish on the counter. But there was no way she was going to tell her boss that she hadn't slept at all last night or that her boyfriend—who, by the way, was an alcoholic—had left town. Terri's answer to everything was a makeover, and she definitely wasn't up for one at the moment.

Instead she just gazed up at her boss with pleading eyes, hoping that for once Terri would display a shred of humanity. Terri scrutinized her for a second, like a parent considering what punishment to dole out to a teenager who just broke curfew, then shook her head. "Just fix it," she said, turning away. "But first take a break and pull yourself together," she called back over her shoulder as she strode away. "Unhappy faces don't sell cosmetics."

Elizabeth closed her eyes, listening to the steady click of Terri's four-inch heels until they faded into the distance. She tried taking a deep breath to help herself relax, but the image of Conner glaring at her in his living room before he took off just kept burning into her mind.

"Hey—can I get some help here?"

Elizabeth's eyes snapped open at the sound of the deep, masculine voice. They didn't get many *guy* customers at the makeup counter. But when she saw who it was, her face relaxed into a relieved smile.

"Hey, Evan," she greeted him, surprised at how

comforted she was just by the sight of him. Their talk at lunch had really helped a lot.

"Sorry," Evan said. "I didn't mean to scare you, but I'm really dying to know what my best colors would be."

She forced a laugh. "Well, I'm on break now, but maybe my boss can help," she said. "You don't want to know how useless I've been tonight."

He raised his eyebrows questioningly.

"Okay—let me rephrase," she said, coming out from behind the counter. "Maybe I don't want to *tell* you how useless I've been."

"Fair enough," Evan said with a smile. He waited while she put away the rag she'd been using to clean the glass counter, and then they walked out of the store.

"So what are you doing here anyway?" Elizabeth asked as they strolled side by side. "You don't seem like the mall-rat type."

"You got me there," he said. "It isn't exactly my favorite hangout." He paused, stuffing his hands into the pockets of his faded cargo pants. "I just thought you might be having a rough night," he admitted. "You know—with what we talked about at lunch and everything. So I figured I'd stop in and check on you—make you take a break or something. And I guess I had good timing."

Wow—he'd showed up just to make sure she was okay? She was really starting to get why all their friends always said Evan was the ultimate nice guy. He had a sarcastic edge to him, but when it came down to it, he was a total sweetheart.

"Well, I'm glad you came," she said. "I mean—thanks."

They walked along in silence for a moment, then Elizabeth turned back up to him. "So where are we headed?" she asked.

He shook a few strands of his shoulder-length black hair out of his face and grinned at her. "It's a surprise," he said. "But not for long," he added as they approached the entrance to Mr. Wiggly, the mall's ice cream parlor for little kids. He took her hand and pulled her inside.

"Oh, I'm not really hu—," Elizabeth started to argue, but Evan dragged her up to the counter.

"Hi," he said to the guy behind the cash register. "I'd like one Mr. Wiggly Kiddie Surprise, please, with—" He turned to Elizabeth and narrowed his eyes. "Chocolate-chip cookie dough?" he asked. She opened her mouth to respond, but he'd already turned back to the guy. "Yep, chocolate-chip cookie dough," he confirmed.

The guy rang up the order and went in the back to prepare it, then quickly returned with the ice cream concoction. The large, shallow bowl, which was decorated all over with little pictures of balloons, crayons, and teddy bears, contained three scoops of ice cream arranged like two eyes and a nose. The "nose" scoop had a big sugar cone sticking out of it, and each of the "eyes" had a bright red cherry in the center. Hot fudge had been drizzled along the top edge of the bowl to make a pair of shaggy eyebrows, and a big piece of strawberry licorice was stretched across the bottom like a mouth. Even though she'd been sure she could never eat another thing, the sight of the sundae actually made her stomach rumble. It was hard not to laugh too. She hadn't eaten one of those things since she and Jessica were little kids.

Evan carried the sundae over to a nearby booth, and Elizabeth followed, sliding in across from him. He handed her one of the long, plastic spoons he'd grabbed at the counter. "Dig in," he said, his expression overly solemn.

She couldn't help giggling as she reached in for a spoonful of "nose" and put it in her mouth.

"It's great, isn't it?" Evan asked.

"Mm-hmm," Elizabeth agreed, her mouth already full with a huge chunk of cookie dough. "Thanks," she said between bites. "For everything," she added, hoping he knew what she meant.

She really didn't know how she would have gotten through this day without him.

"Could you pass the potatoes, please?" Andy asked his dad. Mr. Marsden lifted the yellow serving bowl from the far side of the table and placed it next to Andy.

"Thanks," Andy said.

"You're welcome," Mr. Marsden answered automatically.

"So how was school today?" Mrs. Marsden asked, scooping green beans out of a red dish and onto her plate. He couldn't help wondering how far the soggy, green vegetables would be flung if he startled her by choosing this particular moment to make his announcement. *Conner disappeared, but otherwise it was okay. Oh—and I'm gay.*

"Andy? Did you hear your mom?" Mr. Marsden asked, furrowing his red eyebrows.

"Oh, yeah, sorry," Andy said. His parents must have both had bad days or something—Marsden family dinners weren't usually so tense. Unless he was just imagining the awkwardness in the conversation. "It was fine," he said, moving the green beans around his plate. "I guess Conner split, though," he added, trying not to make it sound too dramatic. The last thing he needed was for his own parents to be fixated on Conner too.

Mrs. Marsden set down her fork. "What do you mean, 'split'?" she asked.

"I don't know," Andy said, shifting on his chair. "He didn't show up in school today, and he left Megan a note that he needed a break or something. I'm sure it's just Conner blowing off steam."

"But if he's still drinking . . . ," Mrs. Marsden began, exchanging a glance with Andy's father. "Well, maybe he just needs to take a day to calm down," she added.

"That's probably it," Mr. Marsden agreed. "Conner's always had a hot head—it's the Irish in him." Andy's father had a habit of citing people's ancestry as a rationale for various behaviors. He didn't mean anything offensive, but it would probably bug some people. Andy couldn't help wondering if his dad would make one of those kinds of comments about him once he knew Andy was gay. Like, *"Andy—you know why you don't like playing contact sports? It's the gay in you—that's what it is."*

Mr. Marsden cleared his throat. "So, Andy, homecoming's coming up pretty soon, right? Do you have a date for the dance?"

Andy choked on the piece of chicken he'd just put into his mouth.

"Drink some water," his mother instructed him, pushing her glass toward him.

Andy took a few sips, and the chicken eased down his throat. "I'm fine," he managed to say, starting to get his breath back. "I just swallowed wrong." He gulped down some more water and then leaned back, feeling more awkward than ever.

"So anyway," Mr. Marsden continued, "about homecoming—are you going to ask that girl you were seeing for a while? Six?"

"No," Andy said, tapping his hand against the edge of the table. "We broke up, remember?"

"Well, we thought maybe you two would have worked things out," Mrs. Marsden said.

How would his parents react if he just screamed *really* loudly? Probably better than if he told them what was actually on his mind. "We weren't right for each other," he said through clenched teeth. "It wasn't serious or anything. No big deal."

"Still, it's a shame," Mrs. Marsden said, reaching for more potatoes.

Why? Andy wondered. Did they already know somehow? Were they just hoping that he'd be with a girl—any girl—or did they really like Six?

He sighed, shoving more chicken in his mouth to distract himself. He knew his parents weren't like that—but as understanding as they were, there was just no easy way to tell them. And even worse—there wasn't anyone around to offer him advice on how to do it.

Welcome to Red Bluff, Conner read, his pulse quickening. The weathered town sign on the side of Interstate 5 was immediately followed by a green exit sign labeled Business District, bearing symbols for food, gas, lodging, and information. Since he'd stopped for breakfast and lunch at diners on the way, Conner definitely didn't need food, but when he looked at the fuel gauge, his Mustang was long overdue.

"It's okay—we made it," Conner said, patting the

brown dashboard above his steering wheel. "We'll get you some gas now." He veered right at the exit, which circled around and sent him shooting straight toward the center of Red Bluff, on the main drag where all the hotels, fast-food joints, and gas stations were packed together, their neon signs lighting up the darkening sky. Conner crossed a bridge that took him over the Sacramento River, then pulled into the first gas station he saw with a supermart.

He stuck the gas nozzle into his tank, chose the cheapest grade available, and then jammed down a lever so it would pump automatically. While his tank was being filled, he jogged over to a pay phone at the side of the convenience store and began thumbing through the phone book. *He probably doesn't even live around here anymore,* Conner thought, flipping to the M's. *If he ever did.*

Deep down, he didn't really expect to find his dad. Sure, there was a glimmer of hope—or maybe apprehension—that made his stomach tighten at the thought, but he'd never even tried to call his dad before, let alone actually track him down. So what were the chances that the guy would still be around here?

McConnell, McCormick, McDaniel, he read, scanning down the page and up to the top of the next column. Then his heart stopped. *McDermott.* There was only one listing, and unless there was another Michael C. McDermott living in Red Bluff, California, it had to be his father. He read the name over and over again, tracing the line of print with his finger, waiting for it to change right in front of his eyes so that he'd realize it actually said Matthew G. or Mildred O.

A loud click from his car snapped him back to attention. The pump had finished, and there were already other cars lined up in back of him, waiting. It was obviously the evening rush hour in Red Bluff. Conner looked back down at the phone book and read Michael C. McDermott's number again. Was his father's middle initial *C*? Conner couldn't remember—if, in fact, he had ever known. And if it was C, was his middle name Conner?

He ignored the honk from the red VW Jetta right behind his Mustang and reached up for the receiver, removing it from its cradle. He held it in his hand a second, then quickly replaced it. This was ridiculous. Just what was he planning to say? *Hey, I was just in the neighborhood, thought I'd stop by. . . .*

The guy in the Jetta honked again, keeping his hand on the horn for longer this time. *Lighten up,* Conner thought, shaking his head. In one swift motion he ripped the McConnell-McDonald page out of the phone book and stuffed it into the back pocket of his jeans. Then he ran inside the supermart and slapped a twenty and a pack of cinnamon gum down on the counter.

"Pump three," Conner told the thin, bleached-blond woman at the cash register. She pressed a few buttons, rang up his gum, and made change without ever looking up. "Thanks," Conner muttered as he headed out, but she only nodded, her leathery, tanned face not showing any emotion. *Time to get a new job*, Conner thought as he jogged over to his Mustang. He unhooked the fuel-pump nozzle and screwed his gas cap back on, raising one hand in a halfhearted apology at the Jetta driver, who didn't seem to care what gesture Conner used as long as he was moving his car. "Friendly town," Conner sneered in his rearview mirror as he pulled away.

Two lights and fifty feet later he stopped again—this time at the Riverside Motel, a two-story, stucco building with red shutters. After seeing his father's name in the phone book, two things had become clear. First, Conner was too tired to attempt any kind of awkward family reunion tonight. And second, unless he wanted to sleep in his car, he probably had to find a room somewhere. If he could even get a room. Was he old enough to rent one? Probably not, but he could pass for older. And judging from the appearance of this run-down place, they probably wouldn't care as long as he had enough money, which he had plenty of from his gig last week.

He parked and climbed out of the car, stretching his legs. The drive had turned out to be closer to six hours than four with all the traffic, and even though he had stopped several times along the way, his muscles still felt tight and cramped.

He headed for the motel lobby, patting his back pocket to make sure his wallet was there—which it was, of course. He pushed open the front door and stepped onto a faded red-and-black-patterned carpet. Directly in front of him was the check-in counter, where a man in a dark blue jacket sat reading a Stephen King book.

Conner shifted his weight from one foot to the other, hoping the noise would get the clerk's attention.

Finally the guy raised his head from the novel. "Can I help you?" he said.

"Um, can I get a room?" Conner ventured, trying to deepen his voice.

The clerk studied Conner for a second, and he made sure not to flinch under the scrutiny. "Okay," the guy said after a moment. He rummaged around under the counter, then placed a small information card and pen in front of Conner. "I just need you to fill out this top part," he said, pointing at the card. "Are you the only one staying?" he asked.

"Yeah," Conner answered, filling in Andy Marsden on the card, then finishing with Tia's address and Elizabeth's phone number. He used his own license-plate number just in case the desk clerk's eyes were better than his thick, black-rimmed glasses suggested. "How much?"

"Sixty-five," the desk clerk told him.

Conner handed the money over, relieved to have a place to crash.

"Here you go," the clerk said, giving him a key attached to an oversized plastic red tag. "That's room 242, around the back and upstairs," he said, already opening his book again and settling back onto his stool. "Have a good night."

"Thanks," Conner said, glad to have the transaction over and done without a hassle. Now he just needed to park his car in the back lot and settle in. It was going to be great to have a little time to himself with no nagging mother to deal with, no sister to feel guilty about, and no friends—or girlfriends—to tell him how *concerned* they were about him.

As he was walking to his car, the bright hotel sign caught his eye, and Conner noticed the words *free cable*. Great—he could lie in bed with the bottle of vodka he'd brought, watch bad movies all night, and wake up fresh and ready to deal with Michael McDermott in the morning.

"Did you make this, Jeremy?" Mrs. Aames asked, taking another big bite of the honey dijon chicken on her plate.

"Nope," Jeremy said, shaking his head. "Trisha and Emma did—I just helped a little." Mr. and Mrs. Aames exchanged a surprised look across the table, then glanced at Jeremy's younger sisters.

"Well," Mr. Aames said, taking a sip of his

drink, "they did a great job. Thank you, girls."

Emma beamed proudly at her father. "We did the asparagus too," she told him.

"And I dribbled the honey on the chicken," Trisha chimed in.

"*Drizzled*," Emma corrected her sister.

"Either way," Mr. Aames said, "it's delicious." He turned back to Jeremy. "So how was practice?" he asked.

Jeremy was about to answer when the doorbell rang. He frowned, wondering who would be showing up at this hour. They were having a late dinner since Jeremy had worked a half shift at House of Java after practice, filling in for Corey.

"I'll get it," he offered, jumping up from his chair. He strode through the living room and into the foyer, taking a quick look out the side window before opening the door.

Jade? He'd been a little surprised when he got the gift she'd left at House of Java. It was nice—but a little weird. Why was the queen of casual suddenly leaving him presents and showing up at his house out of the blue like they were a serious couple?

He shrugged, then pulled open the door, giving her a warm smile. "Hey," he said. "We're actually in the middle of dinner right . . ." He stopped when he saw the way her whole face dropped. "But it's good to see you," he quickly added. "What's up?"

Her black eyes lit up again, and she let out a

giggle. "I think I got the job," she announced. "At the sushi place you told me about. I have an official interview on Sunday, but that Mr. Johnson guy seemed to like me a lot. Isn't that great?"

"Yeah, congratulations," he replied, genuinely happy for her. "And, um, thanks for the stuffed dog too."

The gleam in Jade's eyes grew even brighter, which didn't seem possible. He'd never seen her so *bubbly*.

"I think we should celebrate," she said. "Do something special, you know?"

"Jeremy?" Mrs. Aames called from the dining room.

"I'll be right there, Mom," Jeremy yelled over his shoulder. "I've got to get back to my family," he explained to Jade. "You know—dinner."

"Oh, right," Jade said, nodding. "Just wait one second." She paused, reaching into the shopping bag on the ground next to her, and pulled out a candy bar. "I picked this up for you," she said, handing it to him. "I figured I owed you after all your help, and I remembered this was your favorite snack at work."

"Thanks," he said, feeling awkward. Why did she keep giving him stuff? It wasn't like he did all that much—he just gave her name to a friend of his dad's opening up a new restaurant. She was acting like he won the lottery for her or something. "But it's no big deal, really."

"Yes, it is," she said, tossing her hair back from her face. She was in major flirtation mode—even he could see it, and he was known for being oblivious to that kind of stuff.

"So, um, thanks again, but I really have to get back to my family," he said, casting a backward glance over his shoulder toward the dining room. His dad hated when they weren't all there for dinner.

"Oh, yeah, sure," she said. "Hey, did you realize that tomorrow night will be the two-week anniversary of our first date?" she asked.

Jeremy laughed. "So we'd better do something big," he joked. "I expect more than just candy for that," he said, holding up the chocolate bar she'd given him. A small frown crossed her lips, and he wondered if maybe she thought he was actually taking her seriously. "I'm kidding," he said. "Actually, there's a party at this girl from school's house tomorrow night. I'm going with some friends, and I thought maybe you'd want to come. Then we can always celebrate the anniversary on *Saturday*."

Jade's smile returned. "Sounds perfect," she said. "Just e-mail me the details later. And enjoy your dinner," she said, nodding toward the inside of his house.

"Thanks," Jeremy said, leaning forward to give her a quick kiss good-bye. Jade definitely seemed to be acting different, he thought as he headed back in toward the dining room. But then again, he hadn't actually known her all that long. Maybe he was just overreacting. He'd told himself he was taking it easy this time, so that was probably exactly what he needed to do.

Melissa Fox

Reasons Why Will Should Let Me Visit Him Now

1. He's coming home from the hospital tomorrow, so I won't be seeing him in that stupid gown they make him wear.

2. He needs to get his homework from someone if he doesn't want to get too behind.

3. He's willing to talk to me on the phone, so what's the big deal if I come over?

4. I miss him. . . . Doesn't he miss me?

Great, Conner thought, rubbing his temples. He'd already downed three liters of water from the supermart this morning, but his headache wasn't easing up. He was beginning to think maybe he shouldn't have polished off the entire bottle of vodka last night—partly because the hangover was so bad and partly because he could use another drink about now.

He was parked in his car just down the road from his could-be father's house, which was only about fifty feet from the train tracks of the Southern Pacific Railroad. He'd been sitting here checking out the house—which was so run-down, it could almost be called a shack, but not quite—for a long time now, trying to decide if it made sense to knock on the door. He eyed the beat-up white Ranger truck in the dirt driveway. *So we both drive Fords,* he couldn't help thinking. Talk about pathetic sentimental nonsense—that sounded like something Elizabeth or Tia would say.

Conner glanced down at the clock on his car

radio. One forty-five. He'd been driving around the neighborhood for a half hour now. Pathetic. *It's now or never,* he told himself, jerking his keys out of the ignition. And even though never looked better right now, his only other option was to turn around and go home, which was even worse.

He walked down the cracked pavement that passed for a road on this side of town and up the crooked, redbrick path that led to Michael C. McDermott's front door. Half the shingles on the roof needed replacing, and the white paint on the house was peeling and cracking all over. Still, it could be a decent house if someone put some work into it. And maybe his father had just bought it. It was weird thinking about "his father" doing anything in such a casual way. He'd stopped letting the man even enter his thoughts years ago.

Inhaling deeply, he raised his hand to the door. Weird—his fingers almost seemed to be shaking. Probably from not getting enough sleep. He definitely shouldn't have finished the vodka. If he could just have one sip right now, it would calm his nerves and make this whole mess a lot easier to deal with. Then if Michael C. McDermott wasn't even here, it wouldn't matter. And if he was, and he told Conner to go away and slammed the door in his face, that wouldn't matter either.

He dropped his hand to his side again and considered sneaking away—just hopping in his car and forgetting he'd ever come. If Mr. McDermott had wanted to see Conner once in the last eleven years, he would have known exactly where to find him. So what was the point of knocking? Man, he was getting just as bad as his mom and all his friends—second-guessing every little thing.

Just get it over with, he told himself, raising his fist and knocking three times, forcefully, before he could change his mind. There was a rustling sound from inside, and in a few seconds the door swung open. There, in front of him, stood a scruffy man of about forty-five, with a lean but solid build and graying brown hair. It was strange—somehow he looked totally familiar and still unfamiliar at the same time. It almost felt like seeing some celebrity in person that he'd always known existed and could even imagine in his head but never believed was actually real. When Conner finally met his eyes, his breath caught as he realized he was staring into the same green eyes he'd seen in the mirror all his life. This man was definitely his father.

Suddenly it occurred to him that he should probably *say* something. "Um, Michael McDermott?" he managed.

"Yeah?" his father said, looking back at Conner blankly. He didn't get it—he had no idea that Conner was his son.

The shrill noise of the phone ringing kept Conner from having to come up with a response.

"Can you hold on a minute?" Mr. McDermott asked gruffly.

"S-Sure," Conner stammered, but his father had turned without waiting for an answer. Alone on the front step, he raised his hands to the back of his neck and kneaded his tight shoulder muscles.

This man was his father. It was almost too bizarre to comprehend. And of all the possible scenarios that had run through his mind in the moments before Mr. McDermott had answered the door, Conner realized he had left out one: It had never even occurred to him that his father might not recognize him.

"Thanks again for the ice cream break last night," Elizabeth told Evan as she pulled a few books out of her locker. He'd been waiting there when she got out of last period. It was kind of nice, having someone look out for her. Everywhere she went, Evan just seemed to be around.

"No problem," Evan said. "It was fun."

"Yeah, it was," Elizabeth agreed. "I'm just glad you—" She stopped as a piece of bright orange cardboard fell out of her locker, landing next to her on the floor. All she could do was stare down at the cardboard, her body frozen in place.

"Hey—what is it?" Evan asked. He leaned down and picked it up, flipping it over. She wanted to stop him, to grab it back, but instead she just watched as he skimmed the words she knew by heart. It was the poem Conner had written for her when he was trying to get her back, after she caught him kissing Tia. She wasn't sure how, but she'd forgotten it was still in her locker.

When Evan finished, he glanced back at her with an unbearable amount of pity in his eyes. "I'm sorry," he said softly, placing the cardboard back in her locker. "I shouldn't have read that."

"It's okay," she managed to say, despite the sudden tightness in her throat. *How could I possibly have any tears left in me?* she wondered as she felt fresh ones rising. It was just all of these stupid little things that kept coming out of nowhere and hitting her so hard, forcing her to accept losing Conner all over again.

"Hey," Evan said, stepping closer to her. "I'm here." It felt so good having Evan there. Somehow as her world had spun more and more out of control lately, he'd been the only person to keep her even close to grounded.

"Thanks," she whispered. The tears had retreated, and it was a relief to know she wasn't about to break down and cry for the millionth time. "I don't know how I would have made it through the last three days without you," she said, looking up into his bright, sincere eyes.

A familiar flash of red hair caught her eye over Evan's shoulder, and she realized that Tia and Andy were walking toward them. Instantly she backed up from Evan.

"What's the—"

"Hey, guys," she cut Evan off, waving to Tia and Andy as they approached. She forced a casual, *not* guilty smile. *What is there for me to be guilty about anyway?* It was just a friendly hug. But from the way Tia's eyes narrowed as they darted back and forth between her and Evan, she sensed that Tia was more than a little curious.

"Hey, yourself," Andy said. His hair looked even more wild than usual, and there was a clear uneasiness in his expression. He was obviously really worried about Conner too.

"So what's up?" Elizabeth asked, reaching up to play with the silver heart around her neck. She glanced at Tia, not quite meeting her eye.

Tia frowned. "Nothing new," she said. "Megan told me she begged her mom not to call the cops again, but Mrs. Sandborn said if they don't hear from Conner by tonight, she will. They're both pretty scared, but I guess Mrs. Sandborn realizes that if she does call the police and they find Conner drunk somewhere, he could be in major trouble."

"Well, if they *don't* find him, it could be a lot worse," Elizabeth blurted out.

"Listen, I've gotta go," Andy said, totally ignoring the conversation. "I have an Outdoors Club meeting," he explained.

Maybe he just doesn't handle serious stuff well, Elizabeth thought. He kept bolting whenever things got heavy.

"Wait, Andy, I'll walk with—," Tia started, but Andy was already dashing off down the hall. Tia shrugged, turning back to them. "I guess he really had to go," she said. "Anyway, I have to get to cheerleading practice." She paused, her gaze fixed on Elizabeth. Elizabeth felt her cheeks start to heat up as she wondered what Tia was thinking. "So maybe we can all get together tonight," Tia finally said. "You know, like a support group or something? I'll e-mail you later."

"Yeah, okay," Elizabeth agreed. She was probably just being paranoid. Tia knew there was nothing going on between her and Evan. How could there be?

"That sounded like a good idea," she said to Evan once Tia had taken off down the hallway.

"Yeah, you should go," he agreed. "*After* you take a nap."

She smiled. "Okay, *Mom*," she said. "What about you? Do you think you'll go?"

Evan shook his head. "Can't," he said. "I have a swim meet, and by the time it's over, I'll probably be pretty beat. I think I'll just go home and crash."

"Oh, okay," she said, trying not to think about how disappointed she was over the idea of not seeing him later. "I guess it's about time I made it through a night without you," she half joked.

"Well, actually, I was going to ask if you wanted to do something tomorrow night," he said. "To keep busy, you know. Maybe see a movie or something?"

Elizabeth tensed up, recalling the suspicion in Tia's eyes before. But so what? It wasn't like Evan was asking her on a *date*. He was being her friend, like he'd been doing all week. And there was no reason for her not to let him.

"Sure," she said. "A movie would be great—just not a tearjerker."

"You have my word," Evan pledged, holding up three fingers like a Boy Scout. "No sad movies."

She laughed. "Okay," she said. "So what time?"

"I'll call you tomorrow," he said. "But we should leave early so we have time to pick up some cheap candy before we go to the theater."

Elizabeth tilted her head to the side. "I didn't think you ate candy on a regular basis," she said. "Unless Healthy has some kind of tofu candy I didn't know about."

"No, I don't eat it," he said, grinning. "But you probably do, and I don't want you to go broke before you buy my ticket."

"How sweet," Elizabeth said, swatting at him with one of her notebooks. She knew he was kidding around, but she was still relieved. He wasn't planning on paying for her—which meant it *definitely* wasn't a date.

Obviously. It was crazy to even think that way.

Just relax, Conner told himself, clenching and unclenching his fists as he waited for his dad to return. Yeah, maybe Mr. McDermott didn't recognize him right away, but Conner had been prepared for who he was going to see. His dad had no reason to expect his son to show up on his doorstep like this.

"Sorry about that," Mr. McDermott said as he strode back to the open front door. "Now, what did you need?"

Conner stared into his father's eyes, again overwhelmed at the likeness. "Um—I'm Conner," he blurted out. "Conner McDermott."

Mr. McDermott's bored expression instantly transformed to shock, his eyes widening and his rough skin paling. "Conner?" he said.

Conner nodded, shoving his hands into his jeans pockets. Okay, so now the guy knew who he was. He wasn't slamming the door—but he wasn't inviting him in either.

"Conner," his dad repeated, shaking his head. "Man." He kicked at the peeling carpet by the door. "How's your mom?" he asked.

Conner paused, confused. That wasn't really the first question he'd expected.

"Um, she's fine," he said. As angry as he was at his mom right now, he still felt some strange need to protect her from this guy, to avoid revealing anything about her being an alcoholic and going to rehab.

"That's good to hear." Mr. McDermott scratched his head, finally seeming to focus directly on Conner. "So—how many years has it been anyway? Seven? Eight?"

"Eleven," Conner said flatly.

Mr. McDermott raised his eyebrows. "That long?" Conner nodded. "So you must be what—sixteen now?"

"Seventeen," Conner corrected him. He felt his shoulders tensing all over again. This small talk was getting painful. It was time to get to the important part.

"Look," he said, glancing over his father's shoulder at the messy living room inside. "I'm not here for any kind of major bonding session or anything." He paused, but Mr. McDermott didn't respond. Why would he? The guy probably wanted that as much as Conner did. "The truth is," he continued, "I just had to get out of El Carro for a little while, and I need a place to crash."

"Oh, well . . ." Mr. McDermott hesitated, obviously uncertain how to respond. "Sure," he said, his voice scratching its way out of his throat. He raised his hand to his mouth and coughed a few times. "I'd, uh . . . like to spend some time with you after all these years. But of course you understand—" He coughed again. "You know this can't be . . . permanent," he finished, not meeting Conner's eye.

"That's fine," Conner assured him. "Permanence isn't what I'm looking for."

Mr. McDermott nodded. It was probably a concept he understood pretty well. "Does your mother know you're here?" he asked, frowning.

"Yeah," Conner said without missing a beat. "She's the one who told me where to find you," he lied. His father nodded again, and Conner wondered if his mother actually had known all these years exactly where Mr. McDermott lived. It was possible. But Conner had never asked, and she'd never brought it up—and now, it really didn't seem to matter.

"Well, then. Why don't you grab your stuff?" Mr. McDermott said. "I assume that's your car down there," he said, pointing at the Mustang. Conner followed his father's gaze and nodded. "You can park it in the driveway with my truck and come on in."

"Okay," Conner agreed, walking back down the road to retrieve his car. He was a little surprised that his father hadn't even questioned his lie about Mrs. Sandborn knowing where he was, but he guessed it sort of made sense. He and his father were more or less strangers. How concerned could Conner actually expect him to be? And besides, it wasn't like Conner wanted to be around anyone who was overly interested in his life right now anyway. He needed someone who knew how to leave him alone.

And his father had definitely proved that he was more than capable of that.

"Okay, so it's settled," Travis Hanson said. "We'll do a bottle drive the weekend after homecoming, and we'll use the money to help pay for tent sites at our midyear camp out." There was a general murmur of agreement from the rest of the students in the room. "That's it, then." Travis shrugged. "Oh—and don't forget, you're all invited to a barbecue and bonfire at my house on Saturday."

Andy winced. He definitely wasn't up for any forced socializing—he didn't even feel like hanging out with his so-called close friends.

"Call me if you need directions," Travis finished.

There was a mad rush for the door, and within ten seconds all the members of the Outdoors Club were gone. All of them except Andy, who was still sitting at his desk, trying to scribble over a spot where someone had written *Ken is a big, fat jerk* in capital letters. He wondered momentarily if the writer had meant Ken Matthews or some other Ken, but it didn't really matter. Andy always crossed out all the negative graffiti he saw. Maybe he should put that as an extracurricular activity on his college applications.

General antigraffiti do-gooder or something.

"Andy?" someone called from the doorway. Andy turned to see Six Hanson, Travis's little sister and the casualty of the only dating relationship Andy had ever attempted. "Um, I'm pretty sure Travis said the meeting was over," she said, glancing around at all the empty desks.

"Hey, Six," he said, dropping his pen. "What's up?" He was trying to sound casual, but his voice had squeaked unnaturally on the word *up*.

Six walked back into the room and sat down in a desk across from Andy, tucking her thick, strawberry-blond hair neatly behind her ears. Her deep green eyes were so focused and penetrating that Andy almost flinched. They hadn't really talked since the breakup, and the last thing he needed right now was an in-depth conversation on why their relationship had failed.

"I forgot my bag," she said, pointing at a blue backpack resting on a desk across the room. "What's your excuse?" Andy frowned in confusion. "For hanging out in here all alone," she explained.

Andy shrugged. "Just making the world a better place," he said, pointing at the desk. "You know, getting rid of nasty graffiti."

"What'd it say?" Six asked, leaning in to look. She read the sentence Andy had been trying to cross out. "So maybe he is," she suggested, sitting back in her chair again.

"Maybe," Andy conceded. He wasn't in the mood to debate Ken whoever's positive and negative merits or to defend his reasons for crossing out slanderous statements on desks. For the first time this week, he wasn't in the mood to talk at all. Period.

"Is something wrong?" Six asked, gazing over at him intently. "You seem kind of down."

"No, I'm okay," he said. "It just hasn't been a great week."

"Yeah, I heard Megan talking about what happened with Conner." She shook her head. "What a flake, huh?"

Andy's eyebrows shot up. It was the first time he'd heard anyone refer to Conner like that, as if part of this situation was actually his fault.

"Oh, I don't mean to sound too harsh," she added quickly. "I know he's one of your best friends, and I'm sure he's got some kind of reason. I was just kind of surprised when I heard he ran away. It just sounds so . . . I don't know . . . *flaky*."

Andy stared at her for a minute, then chuckled. "Yeah, I guess," he agreed. Okay, so Six didn't have a clue about everything that was going on in Conner's life, but in a way, Andy had to admit it was kind of nice. At least he wouldn't have to spend the next twenty minutes talking about the evils of alcoholism or how difficult it was for him to have his best friend going through something so major. That would be a welcome change.

Six put her elbows down on the desk and cradled her chin in her hands. "So what else is up with you, Andy?" she asked, watching him thoughtfully. "I mean, I'm sure you're bummed about Conner and all," she continued. "But there's something else going on too, isn't there? You just seem totally out of it."

Andy swallowed hard. How was she able to see right through him like that? It wasn't like they'd dated for a long time or anything. They didn't even know each other that well.

"Do I really look that bad?" he asked, squirming uncomfortably.

Six laughed. "Not bad *hideous* or anything," she told him. "Just worn out and distracted . . . and like there's actually something serious churning around in that head of yours for once."

How was it that this girl he barely knew could read him better than friends he'd known since he was a kid?

Funny, Andy thought. *I never once wanted to kiss her when we were going out, but I could almost do it now.*

Andy picked up his pen and began clicking the ballpoint in and out rapidly. "Yeah, I guess there is something going on," he admitted. "But . . ." He let his voice trail off. Being gay wasn't exactly the kind of topic you were supposed to discuss with an ex-girlfriend.

"But what?" Six prodded. She stared at him with

a mixture of curiosity and genuine compassion, like the way the black Lab puppy Andy'd had as a child used to look at him when he was stuck lying at home on the couch with the flu.

Andy shook his head. "It's nothing," he said. "I mean, it's not even worth talking about."

"Try me," Six pressed. "You know, just because we're not going out anymore doesn't mean we're not still friends. If there's something I can help you with, why don't you let me?" There was something about the way she said it that made it hard for Andy to say no. In fact, there was something about the way Six said *everything* that made it hard to say no. That was the whole reason Andy had started dating her in the first place.

Besides, at least someone was finally interested in listening to him. Wasn't that exactly what he'd wanted all this time?

He stretched his legs out in front of him, gazing down at his desk. "You know how something was just . . . off when we were dating?" he asked her. "Well," he continued before she could respond, "I think it's because I'm gay."

He raised his eyes up to meet hers, anxious. She was still watching him with the same interested, concerned expression—except for some surprise mixed in there too. But definitely no disgust.

"Wow," she finally said. She started to smile. "So that's why you wouldn't kiss me," she said.

Andy rolled his eyes. Maybe Six really wasn't the best person to talk about this with.

"No, seriously," she said quickly. "It really makes me understand things a lot better. But I guess it's kind of the opposite for you, right?"

He gave a half nod. Finally someone recognized how *confusing* all of this was for him.

"So who else have you told?" she asked, settling back in her chair.

"Pretty much all my friends," he said. "Tia, Conner, Liz, Jessica, Maria, Evan—they all know."

"So, has anyone, like, freaked out or anything? Is that why you're upset?" she asked.

"No," Andy said. "They all seem fine. I mean, they keep telling me it doesn't change anything, and we're all still friends and everything, but . . ." He trailed off, shaking his head. "They just don't get it. Things *have* changed—at least for me."

"Have you tried to tell any of them that?" Six asked. She leaned forward, her eyes never leaving his face.

Andy let out a short laugh. "Telling my friends anything right now that doesn't have to do with Conner is totally pointless," he said. "He's going through some pretty big stuff," he explained, "and everyone's basically busy with that."

Six frowned. "Whatever's going on with Conner, it *can't* be bigger than what you're dealing with," she argued in her usual indignant, self-righteous tone. The girl was definitely a fighter.

"Yeah, well, that's not how they see it," he said with a shrug. "I've tried to talk to them about this, but they just don't seem to get it."

"What about your parents?" she asked. "Have you told them?"

Andy shook his head slowly.

"You haven't?" she said, hcr large eyes actually opening wider. "Oh, Andy, you have to."

He almost laughed. Once again Six had jumped right into a subject he'd been trying to get his friends to help him with all week, and he hadn't even had to prompt her.

"Maybe," he said, playing with his pen. "But see, that's what's been driving me crazy. I mean, what am I supposed to say? How do you bring something like that up with your parents?"

"I'm not sure," Six admitted. "But I know you have to do it. I've met your parents, Andy. They're not the kind of people that are going to lose it on you. They'll probably make you feel so much better."

"I know," Andy said, exhaling slowly. "It's just that . . . well, parents have certain expectations for their kids, and I just don't want to, you know. . . ." He stopped, blinking rapidly.

"You're not going to disappoint them," Six told him quietly. He'd actually never heard her voice get that soft.

"Sure, right now they probably think you're going to get married and have kids someday and everything, but that's just because that's what *they* did. And yeah, they might be surprised, but Andy—" She waited until he looked at her. "You're an amazing guy, and they love you. And once you tell them, you won't be so alone with all of this. And you won't feel like you're lying to them by keeping it secret."

Andy took a deep breath and let the air out all at once. Six was right. The worst part of this whole thing had been feeling like he was lying to everyone and having to pretend to be someone he wasn't. And his parents weren't going to hate him or anything. They'd probably be shocked, and it might take them some time to deal with it, but overall, Andy knew they'd do fairly well. And it would be such a relief if they knew.

"Wow," he said, gazing at Six and shaking his head. "Thanks."

Six cocked her head and lifted one shoulder modestly. "I told you I could help," she said with her trademark grin.

"You know," Andy said, a genuine smile creeping onto his face for the first time in days. "If I *were* attracted to girls . . ."

Six reached across the desk and punched him lightly on the shoulder. "Yeah, that's what they all say," she teased, her voice rising back to its normal decibel. She stood and walked over to the desk where her backpack was, grabbing the bag and slinging it over her shoulder. "Good luck with your parents," she said as she headed for the door. "And let me know if you need to talk—anytime."

"Thanks," Andy said, impressed by how cool she'd been with all of this. Maybe he was older than Six, but she was a whole lot wiser.

To: lizw@cal.rr.com, jess1@cal.rr.com, marsden1@swiftnet.com, mslater@swiftnet.com, sandy@cal.rr.com, ev-man@swiftnet.com
From: tee@swiftnet.com
Subject: Friday night support group

Hey, guys—

How about hanging out at Andy's tonight? (Is that okay with you, Andy? I just figured you have that mondo TV in your basement, and maybe we could all just rent a movie or something?) Sound good? I hope so because I don't think I can handle hanging out alone tonight.

Let me know.

—T

To: tee@swiftnet.com, lizw@cal.rr.com, jess1@cal.rr.com, mslater@swiftnet.com, sandy@cal.rr.com, ev-man@swiftnet.com
From: marsden1@swiftnet.com
Subject: re: Friday night support group

Sorry, Tia (and everyone else),
The basement is closed for the night. I, for one, do feel like hanging out alone. Have fun.
Andy

To: tee@swiftnet.com, mslater@swiftnet.com
From: jess1@cal.rr.com
Subject: re: Friday night support group

Hey, gals—

   I'm leaving Evan out because Liz says he has a swim meet and Andy because he's obviously not interested. Was it just me, or was his e-mail a little touchy? Ouch! Also, Megan told Liz earlier that she was just going to hang out at home in case Conner called or something.

   Anyway, the four of us can all hang out here tonight if you want. Elizabeth and I could both use the distraction. If you're in, give me a call and we'll figure out who's picking up the movie and what we need for munchies.

   See you soon,

                     Jess

CHAPTER
Sick of Denying
8

Conner gripped the black receiver of the same pay phone he'd stood in front of the night before. Only this time instead of contemplating dialing an unfamiliar number, he was punching in one that had been etched in his brain for years.

"Hello?" Megan answered on the first ring.

"Sandy, it's—," Conner started, but before he could finish, the operator cut him off.

"This is a collect call from Conner. Will you accept the charges?"

"Yes!" Megan shouted. There was a bit of static, but once it was clear the connection had been made, she started in on him. "Conner—where are you? Are you okay? We've been out of our minds worrying about you! Mom's about to get the cops out looking for you. What are you—"

"I'm fine, Sandy," Conner interrupted her. He was clutching the receiver so tightly that his knuckles had turned white. "Just calm down," he told her. Then he took a deep breath and attempted to take his own advice.

"I'll try," Megan said, exhaling heavily, "but it's kind of hard when I've got no clue where you are or what you're doing."

"I know," Conner muttered. "That's why I called. I didn't want you to worry."

"Not worry?" Megan shouted. Then she paused for a minute. "Where are you anyway?" she asked in a more restrained voice.

Conner contemplated lying to her, but if his mother was really getting ready to call the cops, the truth might be his best bet.

"I'm with . . . my father," he said. The words sounded strange out loud. Especially since he had come to terms with the fact that he didn't have a father years ago.

Megan gasped. "Your *real* father? You mean, you found him? Where?"

Conner glanced around to make sure no one else was nearby. He definitely didn't need the supermart regulars eavesdropping on his conversation.

"In Red Bluff—it's about six hours north of El Carro."

"But how did you—"

"Long story," Conner broke in. It was good to hear his sister's voice, but he was beginning to feel like the conversation had already gone on too long. He had come here to get away, not to start explaining himself all over again—not even to Megan. "Look, I need you to do me a favor," he said.

"Are you coming home?" she asked quietly.

"Yeah," Conner said, "just not right away." It wasn't a total lie—he was certain he'd be going back someday. "But for now I just need you to convince Mom to chill out—not to send the cops out searching for me or to come up here herself or anything."

"But Conner," Megan protested. "She's really worried. She's going to want to know that you're definitely all right and when you're coming back."

"Then you can tell her that I'm fine, and I'll be back by the end of the weekend. I just need some space right now, and besides, my dad seems cool with me hanging out for a while."

"Really? What's he like?" Megan asked. Conner could almost see her green eyes widening with curiosity on the other end of the phone.

"He's okay," Conner answered. "I haven't really talked to him much yet, but he seemed pretty happy to see me." He noticed that the lies were getting easier.

Mr. McDermott had remained more or less expressionless aside from his initial shock. Even as he gave Conner a quick tour of the house and showed him where he could sleep, he had acted more like Conner was a paying guest than his long-lost son. Then after a few minutes of awkward conversation he'd explained that he had to get back to work—he was home on his lunch break—and that he'd see Conner later. So, after a few hours of pointless television, Conner had written his father a quick note and set off to explore the town.

"Well, that's good, I guess," Megan said tentatively. "Are you sure you're okay?"

"I'm fine," Conner insisted, "and I'll be even better if you can get Mom to back down and just wait for me to come home."

There was a pause, and then Megan sighed. He knew it was a tough position to put her in, and normally he'd never do it. But he needed to buy himself a little time, and Megan was the only one who could help him out.

"I'll try," Megan said. "And if she knows you're with your dad, then maybe she'll calm down a little. But you have to *promise* me you're coming home at the end of the weekend."

"I promise," Conner said, wincing. He hated lying to Megan, but he had to do it.

"Okay," Megan said reluctantly. It was obvious that she didn't want to let him go, but Conner was beginning to feel suffocated all over again.

"I'll talk to you soon, okay?" he said. He listened just long enough to hear Megan say, "Okay," then moved the receiver away from his ear and placed it back in the cradle.

Jade looked around the enormous dining room Jeremy was leading her through. A huge cherry-oak table had been pushed to the wall and was piled high with chips, peanuts, pretzels, and other snacks, and there were matching cherry-wood chairs spread out across the rest of the room.

As they entered the living room, music blared from the stereo speakers surrounding the entertainment system in the middle of the room. People were packed into every inch of space, dancing and trying to have conversations over all the noise.

"This is great, Jeremy," Jade yelled, pulling on his hand slightly to get his attention.

"What?" he shouted, glancing back over his shoulder.

Jade just giggled and waved her hand. She pulled him close and gave him a light kiss, then started to dance. Jeremy grinned and joined in.

Finally, she thought. *Just the two of us.* Why did they have to drive over with Jeremy's friends anyway? She'd been so surprised when he came to pick her up and she saw all these random people in his car. Yeah, she was psyched about meeting them, but this was supposed to be a date, not a group thing. And she couldn't help feeling like that Trent guy had been totally grilling her.

Then, when they'd walked into this mansion, Jeremy had immediately run into practically a billion people he knew, so Jade had just stood around by herself while he talked to them. Still, now that they were done with that, she was having an okay time. She'd always loved the atmosphere of parties like this, where everyone was going wild.

When the song ended, everyone clapped and yelled, and Jeremy pulled Jade away from the dance area in the center of the room before the music could start up again. *Oh, good,* Jade thought, assuming he was headed to a quiet spot. *It's about time we had a second alone.*

He dragged her along behind him, then stopped in the kitchen, right near a cluster of people. Jade glanced around, confused. It wasn't exactly the most romantic room in the house. Or the most secluded.

"Jade—this is Katie," Jeremy said, introducing Jade to another new face.

"Hi." Jade forced a smile, giving Katie a once-over. No competition here—the girl was cute, but that was all. Bright little hazel eyes, shiny hair, and an okay body. Jade knew she looked much better in her tight, low-cut green shirt and black miniskirt.

"Hey," Katie replied, her eyes darting back and forth between Jeremy and Jade. Jade took a step closer to Jeremy and interlaced her fingers with his to send the clear message that they were together.

"This is her house," Jeremy explained.

"Oh," Jade said, suddenly overcome with jealousy. She could fit her apartment a few times over in the first floor of this place alone. "It's nice," she said.

"Jeremy, did you see my dad's new TV room?" Katie asked, beaming. "He's got it all set up so he can watch football games with surround sound. It's really cool—it's like you're at the game. Come on, I'll show you." She grabbed Jeremy's free hand and led him away.

Jeremy glanced back over his shoulder and flashed Jade an apologetic smile. He mouthed the words, "I'll be back," and she returned his smile, trying to show she was fine.

Feeling awkward standing there by herself, she made her way back into the living room. What was wrong with Jeremy? Nice guys didn't abandon their girlfriends at parties to go look at some other girl's TV room.

Jade stopped herself. Did she just call herself his girlfriend? Where was all this clinginess coming from? Jeremy had brought her here, and he was leaving with her, and they were spending tomorrow night *alone*. So some rich girl was going after him. That didn't matter—she knew she was the one he wanted to be with.

She strolled over to the small snack table set up by the stereo and grabbed some potato chips, figuring if she was munching, at least she'd look busy instead of just bored.

If anything, she decided, *I should be happy about this.* There was no way she could handle dating a guy who watched her every second and got all freaked out if she talked to someone else. Obviously Jeremy was cool with the two of them doing their own thing for a while at the party.

"Hey—you don't go to Big Mesa, do you?"

Jade glanced up and saw a tall, sandy-haired guy standing next to her, wearing a Big Mesa varsity jacket.

"No, I don't," she said, hoping that wasn't his best pickup line.

"I didn't think so," the guy said, his voice raised so she could hear him above the pounding music. "I'm Bill. I'm the quarterback on the football team."

"Oh, really?" She held back a laugh. Bill was definitely cute, but he was obviously lying to her—or at least stretching the truth. Jeremy's friend Trent was starting quarterback for Big Mesa, and in all their games against Sweet Valley, Jade didn't ever remember hearing the name Bill as a backup quarterback or anything.

"I'm Jade," she said, glancing back toward the stairs. How long did it take for Jeremy to see the stupid TV anyway?

"That's a nice name," Bill said. Jade tried not to roll her eyes. Could this guy get any lamer? "So," Bill continued, leaning in close so he could speak more softly. "You want a tour of the house?"

A tour of the house. Why didn't he just ask her if she wanted to make out?

Just then Jade glimpsed Jeremy and Katie walking into the room together. Perfect timing—Jeremy could come help her get rid of this Bill guy. But when Jeremy caught her eye, he just smiled and waved, then turned to talk to someone else.

Is he totally blind? Jade wondered. Bill was standing so close, he was practically on top of her.

"Come on," Bill said, nodding toward the stairs and gently taking Jade's elbow.

For the tiniest second Jade was tempted. After all, even if Bill wasn't the smartest guy around, he was pretty cute. And Jeremy wasn't exactly paying tons of attention to her. But the idea of actually kissing this guy just didn't appeal to her at all.

"Bill," Jade cooed, blinking up at him. "Do you know Jeremy Aames?"

"Of course," Bill said, frowning. "He's on the team too."

"Mm-hmm." Jade smiled, pulling Bill close and standing on her tiptoes so she could whisper in his ear. "He's my boyfriend," she said.

Bill backed up immediately. "Hey, I'm sorry," he said, blinking nervously. "I had no idea, really."

"And Bill?" Jade continued. "Next time try something just a *little* more original than the whole tour-of-the-house thing—especially when it's not your house."

His cheeks reddened, and he turned and walked away without another word.

Jade smiled to herself. Why did she think she needed Jeremy to get rid of that guy? Like she was just telling herself two minutes ago, it was better that he hadn't rushed over and told Bill to get lost. He could handle watching someone flirt with her because he trusted her now. He knew he didn't have anything to worry about.

And he doesn't, she realized. She really *hadn't* wanted to hook up with Bill—or any of the other cute guys here—at all. She was sick of trying to deny it. For once she was just fine being with one guy. Jeremy was all she needed. And tomorrow night, when they were alone, she was going to let him know exactly how she felt about him.

Teen Girl's Are You Over Your Ex? Quiz
Question #5:

You're sitting in study hall with a few friends when he walks past your table with some girl you've never even seen before practically attached to his side. You:

A. Freak out and confront him right there, demanding that he tell you what's going on.
B. Compare yourself to the other girl, wondering what she has that you don't.
C. Don't even flinch.

Maria Slater: Wait a second—I thought these questions were supposed to be hypothetical. . . .

Jessica Wakefield: I don't have time for this. I have to plan the decorations for the homecoming dance. Besides, Jeremy goes to a different school. This stupid quiz! That's the first time I've thought about him all night.

Well, sort of. What kind of support group is this anyway?

TIA RAMIREZ: WELL, SINCE ANGEL'S IN COLLEGE, THIS COULD TOTALLY NEVER HAPPEN, SO I'LL SAY C—I WOULDN'T EVEN FLINCH—THAT'S GOT TO BE WORTH A FEW POINTS.

Elizabeth Wakefield: I don't have an ex. At least, I don't think I do. I mean, I know the last couple of weeks have been pretty terrible, but he's still my boyfriend, right? I hope he's okay. And I hope he comes back soon. This quiz is definitely not helping me get my mind off things.

Jeremy slowed his car to a stop outside Jade's apartment building and turned down the radio until the soft guitar strain faded into the background.

"Here we are," he said, glancing at Jade. He thought about leaning over to kiss her good night, but he wasn't sure if she'd want him to in front of Stan and Linda. Not that they would have noticed—they'd been giggling together in the backseat ever since he'd dropped off Trent and Stephanie. But still, it was getting late, and he could tell Jade was pretty tired—she had barely talked all the way home.

"Yeah, here we are," Jade echoed in a quiet voice. She stared back at Jeremy for a moment, and he thought maybe he should kiss her, but before he could, she turned abruptly, opening her door and swinging out her legs.

"It was nice to meet you, Jade," Linda said, disentangling herself from Stan long enough to say good-bye.

"Yeah," Stan said. "Nice to meet you."

"You too," Jade said as she started to close the door. She paused, tilting her head at Jeremy. "Aren't you going to walk me to my door?" she asked.

"Oh—yeah—of course," Jeremy said.

"Then you'll have to actually get *out* of the car," Jade teased him. She waved to Stan and Linda in the back, then shut the door and walked around to wait for Jeremy. He fidgeted with his seat belt, finally managing to get it unbuckled.

"Come on, Jeremy," Stan said before he could

open the door. "You have to at least kiss the girl."

Linda laughed, but Jeremy ignored his friend and scooted out of the car, slamming the driver's-side door shut behind him.

"Hey, sorry," he said to Jade as they started walking to her apartment complex. "I would have offered to walk with you, but I thought you just wanted to get going."

Jade rolled her eyes. "Good one," she said.

"No, really, I thought you were beat," he insisted. "I mean, you were so quiet in the car. . . ." He stopped, realizing that maybe her silence on the ride home had nothing to do with being tired. "Are you mad at me for something?" he asked.

Jade shrugged. "No, not *mad*," she said, slowing her pace slightly as they strolled across the courtyard.

"So then—what is it?" he asked, puzzled.

Jade sighed, then kicked a little rock down the path. "I guess I just thought we might get a second alone tonight," she admitted. "I didn't realize we were going to spend the whole time with your friends."

Jeremy frowned. "But I thought you were having a good time," he said.

"I was," Jade answered. "But I've been waiting all night to do this." She stopped walking and stepped closer to him, then wrapped her arms around his neck, pulling his head down to hers. She closed her eyes and pressed her lips to his, gently at first and then harder, more insistently. Jeremy felt his heart rate shoot sky-high as he kissed her back, running his hands through her soft, black hair.

It felt amazing, but he couldn't help thinking how they were only a few feet away from her front door—and there was another couple walking along the sidewalk.

"Mmmm," he said, stepping back slightly. "I'd say it was worth the wait."

"Almost," Jade whispered, pulling him in for another kiss. Jeremy turned his head slightly and pecked her on the cheek instead, then wrapped his arms around her in a big hug.

When he released her, she stared up at him with confusion in her black eyes. "Is something wrong?" she asked.

"No, it's just that . . . well, Stan and Linda are waiting," he said, glancing back at his car. He didn't think it was a big deal, but from the way Jade's head dropped, it seemed like he'd hurt her feelings somehow.

"So maybe you should have dropped them off first," she said. "Did that ever occur to you?"

There was the slightest hint of accusation in her tone, but he knew he had to be imagining it. Jade wasn't the petty type.

"I guess not," he answered. "Stan only lives a couple blocks away from me, so it just made more sense to—" He paused and took a deep breath.

"Look—I'm sorry. I didn't realize you wanted us to be alone. But don't forget, we still have tomorrow night."

Jade's eyes softened a little, and Jeremy thought he could almost detect a trace of a smile.

"And it's our anniversary, right?" he added with a grin, remembering the way she had joked about it yesterday night. Jade was obviously as amused by the idea as he was—her lips curved into a full-fledged smile.

"That's true," she agreed. "And even you wouldn't bring your friends along to celebrate our first anniversary, would you?"

Jeremy chuckled. "No, even *I'm* not that dense," he joked.

"Good," Jade said. "Because I could really use some time alone with you." She stood on her toes and kissed him again, even deeper than before, then pulled away from him abruptly, leaving Jeremy breathless. "You'll have to wait until tomorrow for another one," she said, grinning. "Now, go take your friends home."

She spun around and walked up to her apartment, letting herself in and shutting the door behind her.

Once he saw she was safely inside, Jeremy turned to head back to his car. It really was easy to bring Jade's mood back up—not like with most girls. It was definitely nice to be with someone who didn't take things too seriously.

To: lizw@cal.rr.com, tee@swiftnet.com
From: sandy@cal.rr.com
Subject: Conner!

Hi, Liz and Tia—

   I just wanted to send you a quick note to let you know Conner called. He's with his father in some town called Red Bluff, and he sounds okay. I don't know how he's really doing, but he promised he'd be back by the end of the weekend. Of course Mom freaked out when I told her about it, and she was about to go after him, but I convinced her that Conner would probably just bolt again if he saw her coming or especially if the police get involved. She said at least he's telling the truth— that's where his dad lives. She called and left a message for him, and she told me as long as Conner comes back Sunday night, she'll stay here. (I hope I did the right thing— do you guys think I did?)

   So anyway, that's where things

stand. Thanks for inviting me out, but
I think I'm going to camp out by the
phone for the rest of the weekend in
case he calls again. I'll talk to you
both soon.

Megan

Andy Marsden

<u>How to Tell My Parents I'm Gay</u>

1. Hey, Mom and Dad, do you remember how when we were little, Tia always used to make me and Conner play Getting Married with her? And half the time she'd be the bride marrying Conner and I'd be the minister, and then the other half of the time she'd make me marry Conner so that she could perform the ceremony? Yeah, well, as it turns out, that whole thing hit a little closer to home than any of us realized at the time. . . .

2. You know that TV show with the gay guy and his best friend, that really attractive girl? Well, don't you guys really like the gay guy? I mean, he's really nice, isn't he? And funny. Yeah, well, anyway, I was just thinking— wouldn't it be nice if I could be like him?

Okay. So these suck. That's all right. I can do this. I know I can. I just have to get myself psyched up for it, and I'm sure everything will come together perfectly. Yep. That's exactly what I'm going to do.

First thing in the morning.

"Andy, you're up early," Mrs. Marsden said as Andy shuffled into the kitchen on Saturday morning, still in his plaid pajamas.

"Yeah," he answered, "I guess so." He glanced at his dad, who stood in front of the range, scrambling eggs. His mom sat at the table, drinking her coffee and reading the paper. "I couldn't really sleep."

"Are you coming down with a cold?" Mr. Marsden asked, tossing the light yellow eggs around the cast-iron skillet like an old pro.

Andy shook his head. "No, I've just got a lot on my mind."

Mrs. Marsden folded her paper and studied his face with her mom radar. This was good. Maybe if he just hinted at it long enough, they'd ask all the right questions and drag it out of him. Then he wouldn't have to spend all morning fumbling for the right words.

"What is it, Andy?" his mother asked, leaning forward. "You seem really upset. Did something happen to Conner?"

139

Andy sighed. It was a natural question, but if he let them go down that path, they'd never get around to talking about what was really bothering him. "No. I haven't heard anything new. For all I know, he could be home by now."

"Do you think he is?" Mr. Marsden asked. "Do you want to go over and check? Would that make you feel better?"

Andy shook his head. "That's not what's bothering me, Dad," he said, walking over and sinking down in the chair across from his mom. "Not even close."

Mrs. Marsden frowned, her concern obviously increasing. "Well, then, what is it?" she asked.

Andy's eyes flicked from his mother to his father and back to his mom. He still didn't have the slightest clue how to tell them.

"You know you can tell us anything," Mrs. Marsden said. "Are you in some kind of trouble?"

I wish, Andy thought. If he were running from the mob or facing jail time for grand-theft auto, he'd probably have an easier time getting the words out.

"No, not trouble, really," he said. "It's just that, well, you remember how when we were little, Tia used to—" He stopped, looking down at his socks. "Dad, I think maybe you should sit down," he said.

Mr. Marsden shut off the burner and came over to the table, sitting between Andy and his mom.

"Whatever it is, Andy, we're here for you," Mrs.

Marsden said. "You know that, don't you?"

"Yeah, I do," he answered, but he couldn't help feeling that if they knew what he was about to say, they might decide this was one of those times they should just let a subject drop.

"Just come right out with it, Andy—that's always the easiest way," his father encouraged him.

Both of his parents were on the edges of their seats, waiting for him to continue, and Andy knew that if he was going to do this at all, now was the time. He swallowed hard and tried to hold his mother's gaze without glancing away.

"I don't know how to say this," he began, shaking his head. "I mean, I don't think there's an easy way, so I'm just going to do it." He brought his hands to his head and clenched fistfuls of red curls, unable to resist breaking eye contact with his mom at the last second. "I've been doing a lot of thinking lately, and . . . well, the thing is . . . I think I might be . . . gay."

Aside from Mrs. Marsden's quick intake of breath, the kitchen was totally quiet, with only the sound of crackling eggs on the still hot frying pan filling the air. Andy didn't dare look up. What were his parents doing? Exchanging disappointed glances? Staring at him like he was a freak? Crying? Andy was certain a full minute had passed without anyone saying anything, but he felt like he was glued in place, and he didn't want to be the first person to speak. Then he felt his mother's arm on his back, followed by his father's hand on his shoulder.

"Oh, Andy," Mr. Marsden said. "I had no idea. I mean—I have to admit . . . I'm surprised."

"I—I don't know what to say," Mrs. Marsden added. "It never even occurred to me that . . . well, that you might be gay." She rubbed Andy's back soothingly, just as she always had when he was little. Probably because she didn't know what else to do.

Andy sat still, taking in the reassuring gestures from both his parents. They weren't offering to drive him to a gay-pride parade, but they obviously weren't upset with him either. Just shocked, which was what Andy had expected.

"How—How long have you known?" Mrs. Marsden asked. "I mean—well, I don't know exactly how this works, but—"

"I think what your mother's trying to ask," Mr. Marsden interrupted, locking eyes with his wife, "is how long have you been trying to tell us? Or trying *not* to tell us, as it may have been?"

"Yes." Mrs. Marsden nodded vigorously. "That's exactly what I was trying to say."

"Um, I don't know, really," Andy said. "I guess I've been thinking about it for a while, but it's kind of something I'm just starting to deal with myself. I mean, I don't even really understand what it means or what comes next—I just know that this feels like what's right. Like it's part of who I am."

"Oh, Andy," Mrs. Marsden said, leaning closer to

him. "I'm just so glad you came to us. I'd hate to think of you trying to handle something like this alone. And you know that you can count on your father and me for *anything* you need."

"Your mother's right," Mr. Marsden chimed in. "This will take time to understand—for all of us. But we are here for you, and we love you, and there's nothing in the world that could change that."

Andy felt hot tears welling up under his eyelids and blinked rapidly a few times to keep them in check.

"Thanks," he choked out. "I guess I just thought you'd be . . . disappointed."

"Never," his father said firmly. "There's no way you could ever disappoint us."

"All we want is for you to be happy, Andy," Mrs. Marsden agreed. "And that means being true to yourself."

Andy gazed gratefully back and forth between his parents. Six had been right. Telling them had been the right thing to do, and even though they were shocked, they were managing this amazingly well.

Seeing all the love in their eyes made him feel like a huge weight had been lifted off his shoulders—one he'd been carrying for longer than he'd even realized. And even though he wasn't sure what to do next, at least he knew that no matter how much things changed, there were some things that he could always count on. Most important, his parents.

Jade plopped down in the orange plastic chair in the middle of the mall's food court, setting her bags on the floor. She hadn't done a lot of shopping—just enough to buy a killer black dress for tonight's date with Jeremy and a new pair of earrings—but she was still worn out.

"Hey, Jade—what's up?"

Jade turned to see Annie Whitman pulling up a chair from a nearby table.

"Oh, hi, Annie," she said, trying not to sound annoyed. Annie was nice and everything, but she could talk forever, and Jade didn't want to get trapped in the food court all afternoon. Still, Annie was one of the only girls on the cheerleading squad who was still talking to Jade, so it was a good idea not to be rude to her.

"So what did you get?" Annie asked, pointing at the bag at Jade's feet.

"Just a dress," Jade said with a shrug. She pulled out the black dress she had fallen in love with at first sight and held it up for Annie to see.

"That's gorgeous!" Annie gushed, her green eyes lighting up. "Is it for the homecoming dance?"

"Actually, no. It's for tonight," Jade said, tucking a strand of black hair behind her ear. "I have a date with Jeremy."

"Oh, right, Jeremy," Annie said, grinning. She started to unwrap her sandwich. "How are things going with him anyway?"

"Pretty good," Jade answered, folding the dress and placing it carefully back into the bag.

"Just *pretty good?*" Annie asked, narrowing her eyes. "You don't sound very excited."

Jade bit her lip. After Jeremy had left last night, Jade had started second-guessing things, wondering whether he really was serious about her or not. Now that she knew what she wanted, she had to be absolutely sure that she had him pegged right as the settling-down kind of guy. Actually, she wouldn't mind getting some advice on the subject, but she wasn't sure if it was a question she wanted to bounce off Annie.

Annie took a big bite of her chicken-wrap sandwich, and Jade's stomach grumbled, but she reminded herself of her promise not to buy anything to eat here. The food was way overpriced, and this dress had already pushed her over budget.

"So what's the deal?" Annie asked after she'd swallowed.

Jade studied Annie's green eyes and friendly smile. She did look sincerely interested, and it might help to get another point of view. Jade wasn't exactly overflowing with girlfriends lately.

"Well, it's kind of silly," Jade admitted. "But last night we went to this party, and when Jeremy took me home afterward, he was barely interested in . . . you know. I mean, he wasn't even going to kiss me good night until I practically pulled him out of the car." Jade leaned closer and lowered her voice. "And even then *I* had to kiss him."

Annie frowned. "Is that it?" she asked. "That's why you're upset?"

"Well, yeah," Jade said. "Don't you think it's a little weird that he wasn't more anxious to kiss me? I mean, every other guy I've ever dated has always been more excited at the end of the date than at the beginning."

"I know what you mean," Annie said. A strange, almost sad expression came over her face. "But honestly, I think it's a good sign that Jeremy held back a little."

"You do?" Jade asked, crossing her legs under the table.

"Oh, yeah," Annie replied, nodding. "Look," she continued more seriously, "it's no secret that I dated a bunch of guys in the past. Last year . . . well, there were a lot. And believe me, plenty of them had no problem jumping all over me. But what I learned is that the ones who want to take things slow are the ones who really like you."

"You think so?" Jade asked, wrinkling her nose. It sounded a little weird.

"Definitely," Annie said. "And didn't you say you had a date with Jeremy tonight too?" Jade nodded.

"Well, then you've got nothing to worry about," Annie continued. "Do you really think he'd keep asking you out if he didn't like you? Jeremy was probably just trying to make sure you didn't get the wrong idea. He wants a *girlfriend*, not just someone to have fun with and drop the next day."

Jade felt a smile creep onto her face. Suddenly she was anxious to get out of the mall and start getting ready for her date. "Thanks, Annie," she said, gathering her things and standing up. "I should get going."

"No problem," Annie said. "Have fun tonight," she added, smiling.

"I will," Jade said before turning to leave. Now that she was convinced that Jeremy was as serious about her as she was about him, she was more motivated than ever to make their anniversary celebration perfect.

"I'll get it," Elizabeth yelled the second she heard the doorbell ring on Saturday afternoon. It was just about time for Evan to pick her up, and for some reason she felt weird about Jessica or her parents letting him in.

She grabbed her purse from the table next to her and jogged down the hall, then pulled open the front door, ready to follow Evan straight out to his car. But instead of Evan, Tia stood on her front step.

"Tee?" she said, frowning. "What are you doing here?"

"You were expecting Brad Pitt?" Tia joked, stepping right in. "Hey, I know you said you might have to hang out here today, but I thought I'd stop by anyway to see if you'd changed your mind. Did you get Megan's e-mail?"

"Actually, no," Elizabeth said, glancing past Tia outside. No sign of Evan's car, but he would be showing up any minute. "Why?" she asked, focusing on Tia again. "What did she say?"

"Conner called her last night," Tia explained, "and he told her he's with his dad up North. Megan said he's staying the weekend, but supposedly he's coming back tomorrow, although I'm not totally sure—I mean, he may have just said that to make Megan feel better, you know? It's not like Conner is the most reliable person in the world these days, but still, I can't see him lying to his sister, and at least we know where he is, right?"

Tia finally took a breath, and Elizabeth tried to process everything she'd just blurted out. Conner was okay—for now. With his dad. When was the last time he'd seen him anyway? She hadn't even known they were in touch. How much more of her boyfriend's life had she been shut out of?

"So, you know, maybe he really just needed a break and he'll be back tomorrow," Tia said, flipping her long, dark hair back from her face. "That would be such a relief, wouldn't it? It would be like the whole thing was just a bad dream or something."

Elizabeth winced. "Well, I don't know. I mean, no matter what, we know he has a serious drinking problem—"

"Yeah," Tia interrupted, letting out a long sigh. "I know, I know. That's why I thought it would be good for us to get out tonight, and I thought we could drag Andy along too. I mean, if we don't do something, we're all just going to sit around thinking ourselves into a hole. So what do you say? Ice cream? Coffee?" She smiled. "Coffee ice cream?"

Elizabeth's stomach sank. She had really wanted to avoid mentioning Evan to Tia, especially after the look Tia had given her in the hallway yesterday afternoon. But it seemed like she was going to have to explain about their plans. She glanced down at her watch—he really would be pulling up anytime now.

She took a deep breath. "Actually," she said, "Evan's coming over soon, and we're going to a movie."

Tia's eyes instantly narrowed. "Evan?" she said, crossing her arms over her chest. "You guys have been spending a lot of time together lately, haven't you?"

"Well, yeah, I guess," Elizabeth said, shifting her weight from one foot to the other. So what if she and Evan had hung out a lot this week? They'd spent almost all the time talking about Conner. "Evan and I are just friends," she couldn't help adding.

Tia's eyebrows shot up. "Oookay," she said. "And is he with you on that?"

"Yeah, of course," Elizabeth said. In a rush she felt indignant that Tia would stand there, hinting around about her doing something wrong after everything that had happened with Tia and Conner. "And you know what?" she continued. "When I say I'm just friends with a guy, I actually mean it."

Tia gasped. "Excuse me?" she said. "And just what is that supposed to mean?"

"It means that you have no right to lecture me about how to behave with guy friends," Elizabeth snapped.

"I'm not lecturing you," Tia shot back. "I'm just pointing out that ever since Conner left, you've been clinging to Evan. I mean, that little *moment* in the hallway looked pretty intense from where I was coming from."

"We were just talking," Elizabeth said, gritting her teeth. She hadn't even realized all the resentment was still there, but now that they'd started this, it was all rising to the surface. "The way friends are supposed to talk to each other when things get rough," she continued. "But I can see how you might get that confused. Especially since you seem to think it's okay to make out with your friends, whether they have girlfriends or not. And whether those girlfriends happen to be your supposed friends or not too."

"Oh, *please*," Tia said, her eyes flashing. "Can't you give that a rest already? If you weren't always so holier-than-thou, Conner never would have come to me in the first place."

Elizabeth swallowed back the hurt from what Tia was implying. "Conner didn't come to you," she said quietly. "You were lonely because Angel was gone. And you were jealous that my boyfriend was still here."

"Is that what you think happened?" Tia shot back, her voice getting louder. "You think *I* went after Conner? Do you really believe that he had no role in that whole mess?" She paused. "You know what? I'm not going to defend myself anymore. This isn't about Conner; it's about you and *Evan*. And how the second your boyfriend disappears, you have to start something up with one of his best friends."

"There's *nothing* going on with me and Evan!" Elizabeth practically shouted. To her horror, when she glanced out the still open door, she saw Evan coming up the walk.

Tia followed her gaze, then turned back to her, glaring. "Yeah, right," she said. "I just wonder what you guys will tell Conner when he does come back," she said.

And before Elizabeth could respond, Tia stormed out the door.

Jade Wu

Jeremy—

I know we've only been seeing each other for two weeks, and I know I haven't been the world's best girlfriend so far, but that is definitely going to change. That's why I made you this card—because there are a few things I need you to know, and I kind of feel like a dope saying them out loud.

I know it's mushy, but I really care about you. You're the only guy I've ever met that's actually made me want to get serious. So I guess what I'm really trying to say is that I'm glad we finally got together—as an official couple, I mean. And I hope we'll be celebrating a lot more anniversaries together. You're really cool, and I'm psyched to be your girlfriend.

—Jade

Jessica Wakefield

Okay, so I didn't hear the whole argument between Jia and Liz from the kitchen, but I did hear Conner's name a few times — big surprise there — and I think I heard Evan's too. Now, that was weird. Then when I came out and saw Evan himself here, picking up <u>Liz</u> to go out, I said it looked like he was dating his way through our family and that he'd be dating Mom next. Elizabeth practically bit my head off. At least Evan thought it was funny. But the point is, she didn't. Which makes me wonder if maybe there's more going on there than Liz is willing to admit. And honestly, even if Evan and I are just friends now, I'm not sure how I feel about that.

CHAPTER
Holding Out Hope
10

Jeremy felt the front pocket of his khaki pants for the familiar jingle of car keys. "Check," he muttered to himself. He started ticking off the other things he needed to bring with him on his date with Jade. *Wallet, watch, sunglasses . . .* he looked around his room, scanning the top of his dresser and his desk. Why did it seem like he was forgetting something?

Oh, right, he remembered, dropping his wallet on the bed and rifling through his desk drawers for a piece of paper. He'd almost completely forgotten that this was supposed to be some kind of joke anniversary date. Jade would probably bring him another cute gag gift, like the little stuffed dog she'd left at House of Java, so he wanted to be prepared with something for her too.

After a few minutes of rummaging through his desk, he finally found a piece of green construction paper left over from one of Trisha's class projects.

"Perfect," he said. He folded the paper in half, then took a black permanent marker from his top desk drawer and drew a heart on the front with his and Jade's initials inside and one of those true-love-forever symbols he remembered girls making all over everything when he was in junior high. On the inside, Jeremy used the same black marker to scribble a quick note, and then he made another goofy heart design on the back.

He held the card at arm's length and admired his work. *Not bad for the last minute,* he thought. And it was certainly good enough for a fake anniversary celebration. Jade would think it was hysterical. He just had to make sure she could tell he was goofing around with the "true-love" stuff since he knew the idea of actually being a serious couple would freak her out way more than it would even bug him at this point.

Jeremy Aames

Dear Jade—

*Happy anniversary! These have been
the best two weeks of my life—or was it
three? Whatever. Let's do it again
sometime.*

—J

"Stupid calculus," Andy muttered, crossing out the last three lines of the equation he'd been working on. Why couldn't Elizabeth have been in study hall when he needed her?

Suddenly he heard the screen door at the back of the kitchen open and slam shut, followed by Tia's familiar voice babbling as she approached.

"Andy! You're not even going to believe what Elizabeth said to me!" Tia ranted, stalking into the living room and positioning herself right in front of the coffee table, where he was trying to do his homework.

"I went over there to see if she wanted to do something, but she already had plans—with Evan, of all people. So I just happened to mention that they'd been spending a lot of time together this week, and she totally went off on me—accusing me of going after Conner and trying to steal him away from her, when that wasn't how it happened at all, and—are you hearing this?"

She stopped, staring at Andy as if she were waiting for him to stand up and scream with shared indignation at the injustice of it all.

But Andy was done taking all of this without speaking up. He set his math book and pencil down on the floor next to him and sat up straight, meeting Tia's eye.

"Do you have any idea what I did this morning?" he demanded. "Oh, wait—you couldn't possibly," he continued, "because you haven't listened to a word I've said lately unless the word happened to be Conner's name." He paused. "Well, this morning I told my parents I'm gay."

Tia blinked, her shoulders slumping.

"That's right," he went on. "I sat down at breakfast and told them—do you know how hard that was for me? Do you know how hard this *entire week* has been for me?"

Tia shook her head.

"You know why you don't?" he asked. "Because the Tia-Liz-Conner show is the only thing you can ever talk about, and I am *sick* of it."

All the emotions Andy had been holding inside for weeks now pushed their way to the surface, and he couldn't hold any of it back. "I really needed you this week—all of you—but no one was there for me. Do you know who finally noticed there was something wrong and took the time to actually find out what it was?"

Tia pressed her lips together, her face paling.

"Six!" he exclaimed, jumping up and starting to pace across the room. "Six Hanson! A girl I dated for about three minutes. What does that say for the rest of my friends? Not much." He sank back onto the couch, feeling completely drained.

"Andy, I—I'm really sorry," Tia said quietly. She moved closer and sat down next to him. "I don't know what to say."

That's a first, Andy couldn't help thinking.

"You're right, you know," she said, picking up the throw pillow at the end of the couch and turning it over in her hands. "I have been totally self-absorbed. I mean, all this stuff with Conner—"

Andy sighed. If she started talking about that now, he was going to kick her out.

"—but that's no excuse," she said quickly. "I should have listened to you. You've always been there for me, and I wish I could have been here for you. I'm really, really sorry."

Andy swallowed. He could tell that she honestly felt bad. He'd let her have it big time, and it seemed like maybe he'd finally gotten through.

"Do you think maybe we could, I don't know, go somewhere and talk?" she asked, her tone way more cautious than usual.

He squinted down at the textbook lying on the carpet. He *could* use a break from his math homework—but he didn't want this to turn into another venting session for Tia.

"I promise this will be all about you," she assured him, scooting closer on the couch. "We don't even have to say the *C* word at all," she added, the corners of her mouth twitching into a hint of a smile.

Andy laughed. "Okay," he said. "Thanks."

"Good." Tia nodded, then stood up. "Come on," she said, reaching for his hand to pull him up. "Let's get out of here. I want to hear how it went with your parents and everything."

This time it seemed like she actually meant it. He hoped.

"So where are we going?" Jade asked, glancing over at Jeremy's khaki pants and blue T-shirt for the eighteenth time since she'd gotten into his car. Why was he dressed so casually? Wasn't this supposed to be an anniversary celebration? *Maybe his good clothes are in the trunk,* Jade thought, still holding out hope that he was going to surprise her at the last minute.

"Is First and Ten okay?" Jeremy asked without taking his eyes off the road. Jade smoothed out the skirt of her black dress and slanted her legs to the side so her platforms rested smoothly against each other. He had to be joking. First and Ten? For a romantic dinner?

"Yeah, sure," Jade said, figuring she'd play along with the joke. Now she knew he must have nicer clothes stashed in the trunk. *What kind of guy would take his girlfriend to a sports bar for—*

But even as the thought was forming in her head, Jeremy put on his turn signal and swung down the side street leading to the restaurant where she used to work. Jade frowned, staring down at the tan dashboard as he cut the ignition.

"Ready?" Jeremy asked, pulling open his door. It

was unbelievable. He was really getting out. And he expected her to get out too. Jade wanted to yell, "Okay—joke's over," but she was starting to get that Jeremy wasn't kidding.

"Are you coming?" he asked, poking his head back in.

"Um, yeah," Jade said, fingering the silver necklace around her neck. She couldn't help feeling like she was a little overdressed for First and Ten, but if she was, it was totally lost on Jeremy.

They headed for the entrance, which was surrounded with pennants for various sports teams and huge neon beer signs. Was this really going to be the place where Jeremy told her he wanted to be a couple—officially? It couldn't be. Why hadn't he taken her somewhere special?

Then it hit her. *He must have something else planned*. That had to be it. After all, Jeremy couldn't afford a fancy dinner. They'd have their burgers, then he'd take her to some really romantic place afterward, like Crescent Beach. She just needed to relax and go with this. Then later, when the timing was right, she would give him the card she had hidden in her purse, and they'd go riding off into the sunset. Or live happily ever after. Or whatever it was that happy couples did—she certainly wasn't an expert on that. But she would be soon—she could feel it.

*   *   *

"Sorry," Elizabeth hissed, jerking her hand out of the bucket of popcorn after brushing up against Evan's fingers. Her night of relaxing and getting her mind off things was turning into a total disaster. Instead of feeling comfortable and easy with Evan like she usually did, she'd been on edge all night— keeping her arms glued to her sides to avoid touching his elbow on the armrest and almost jumping out of her seat every time they reached for popcorn at the same time. She was more tense now than she'd been all week.

Thanks to Tia. And Jessica. That stupid comment about Evan dating their whole family hadn't helped at all. At least Evan hadn't actually overheard the end of her fight with Tia, though. Or if he had, he wasn't saying anything about it.

Evan leaned toward her, obviously getting ready to whisper something in her ear. She felt a shiver run down her back as she curved her spine unnaturally to keep her body as far away from his as possible.

I've got to get a grip, she told herself.

"Hey," Evan whispered. Elizabeth glanced up at him, not meeting his gaze.

This is not a date; this is not a date, she repeated as she reluctantly bent her head to hear him.

"You know, Liz, I've been thinking a lot," he started. Every muscle in her body stiffened. She couldn't believe what she was hearing. What if Tia and Jessica had seen something she'd totally missed?

What if Evan really did think this was more than a friendly thing? "And I've come to an important conclusion," Evan continued. "This movie sucks."

Elizabeth looked back at him blankly for a second and then burst into relieved giggles. She cupped her hand over her mouth, trying to stop laughing, but she couldn't. All the tension that had built up inside her just came out at once, and everything suddenly seemed overwhelmingly funny. Evan started to chuckle along with her, which caused a few people to shush them, but after a minute Elizabeth was able to get herself under control.

"It really does," she finally whispered back to Evan. "I mean, aren't they ever going to get off that train? And I could really go for a different camera angle."

The woman in front of them turned around and gave Elizabeth a dirty look, which for some reason just made her want to laugh again. Instead she leaned in closer to Evan.

"She has to be getting something out of this movie that we're missing," Elizabeth muttered. "Like, I don't know, the *point*."

Evan shook with silent laughter, and Elizabeth sank down in her seat, trying to be quiet. But somehow it wasn't working—she couldn't even concentrate on the stupid movie anymore. She could barely contain herself from bursting into another fit of giggles.

"Let's get out of here," she whispered to Evan.

He nodded, and they both stood and squeezed by the other people in their row. Once they made it to the aisle, they ran up to the exit, collapsing in laughter as soon as they were outside the theater doors.

"You know," Evan said as they made their way through the lobby, "for a really bad comedy, it did make us laugh a lot. Maybe we should go back in and watch the rest."

Elizabeth groaned. "I don't think that's a good idea," she said, wiping away the tears that had come from laughing so hard. The first happy tears she'd had in a long time, she couldn't help noting. "Let's just get out of here before one of the ushers catches up to us and asks us never to come back."

"Deal," Evan said, heading for the outside door.

"Oh, and Evan?" Elizabeth said, catching him by the wrist. "Next time *I'm* picking the movie."

Andy Marsden

Okay, so maybe I'm still not getting the main-character treatment that I deserve with <u>all</u> my friends, but my parents sure didn't treat me like a walk-on. And at least Tia finally came around. She actually <u>listened</u> to me talk for the whole time we were at House of Java, and she kept her promise—no discussion of Conner. Unbelievable. So really, things could be a lot worse.

I don't get it, Jade thought as Jeremy pulled into a spot outside her apartment building. There hadn't been any romantic place after dinner—just First and Ten. And Jeremy hadn't said anything about their relationship or anything serious at all. Was it possible that she had gotten everything all wrong?

"I had a good time," Jeremy said, leaning over to kiss her. Jade turned her face so that Jeremy's lips caught her on the cheek instead of the mouth.

"Are you okay?" he asked, pulling back.

"Yeah, fine," she said. She wasn't about to make a big deal out of it when she wasn't even sure if there was anything to make a big deal out of. Maybe Jeremy didn't feel the same way she did after all. Or maybe something had happened with his family that had thrown the entire night off, and he was too distracted or upset to talk about it.

"So . . . I'll talk to you tomorrow?" she said, still waiting for him to do or say something *more*.

"Yeah, and you can let me know how your job

167

interview went," he said, his hands on the steering wheel.

"Oh, right," Jade agreed. She sat there another minute, wondering what to do with her card. Obviously she couldn't give it to Jeremy now—not after this disaster of a date. "Good night," she said finally, opening her car door and sliding out her legs.

"Oh, wait," Jeremy called just as she was about to stand up. "I almost forgot." He leaned over and opened his glove compartment, pulling out a small piece of heavy paper. "Just a little something for our *anniversary,*" he said, emphasizing the word in a strange way.

Instantly Jade brightened. "Thanks," she said, feeling herself blush. "I have something for you too." She fished around in her purse for the card she'd made, then handed it to him. "I did it on the computer," she explained. "We have one of those greeting-card programs. . . ." Jade let her voice trail off, realizing that she was actually *babbling*. What was happening to her?

"Thanks," Jeremy said, starting to open it.

"Wait," she blurted out. "I'm kind of embarrassed to have you read it in front of me." Jeremy scrunched his eyebrows together. "I know, it's stupid," she continued, "but can you do me a favor? Can you just, like, not read it until you get home or something? I'd feel a lot better that way."

"Okay," Jeremy said, still looking puzzled. "So

remember, let me know how the interview goes," he said as Jade got out of the car.

"I will," she called back. "And Jeremy? Thanks," she said, holding up the card he had given her. She couldn't wait to get inside and read what he'd written. He was probably just too shy to say all that mushy stuff out loud, like she was.

"Um, sure," Jeremy said. Jade beamed at him, then turned and ran across the courtyard to her apartment. As soon as she was inside the door, she dropped her purse, kicked off her shoes, and stared down at Jeremy's card. The heart on the front was kind of cute in a silly way, but she was certain the inside would be serious.

She ripped it open, scanning the words. When she reached the end, her throat suddenly got very tight. *"Let's do it again sometime"*? What was that supposed to mean? She flipped the card over to the back to see another childish heart. Was that it? It couldn't be.

She read the message again, certain she must have missed something, but she hadn't. What was he saying—that this was all a big joke in his mind? That *she* was a joke? Jade's heart sank as she read the message again and again. How could he do this to her? *How could he—*

Suddenly Jade jerked up her head as she remembered the card she'd given *him*. She ran to one of the front windows and looked out, but his car was long gone. She walked back to the sofa, sinking down onto the edge, still clutching his pathetic card. She'd written all of that stuff to Jeremy about how much she cared about him, and he'd given her—*this*.

Who was she kidding anyway, thinking she could actually be someone's girlfriend? She never should have broken her rule and actually let herself get attached to someone. It was a mistake she was definitely not going to let happen again.

Clenching her jaw, Jade walked over to the sink and splashed cold water on her face, toweling it off with a fresh washcloth. No way she would cry over this.

She glanced at the clock over the stove. It wasn't even that late—still early at the Riot. And Jade was sure there were tons of guys there who could help her forget all about Jeremy Aames.

"So, what do you do for work anyway?" Conner asked, watching his father across the red vinyl booth in Roger's Old Tyme Saloon. He figured he had a right to ask since Mr. McDermott had spent all of Friday and most of Saturday doing whatever it was he did.

Conner had barely spent any time with his father at all—which was fine with him. He wasn't looking for a new buddy anyway. But maybe his dad had finally felt like he should exchange a couple of words with his son because he had brought

Conner to this local hangout for a late dinner tonight.

"I work at the brickyard just over the tracks," Mr. McDermott said, taking a sip of his beer. "It's not much, really, but it pays the bills."

"Oh," Conner said. "Masonry's cool." He'd seen people lay bricks before, and there was a bit of artistry to it. Maybe that's where his creativity had come from—after all, he certainly hadn't inherited it from his mother.

"No, I don't actually do anything with the bricks," Mr. McDermott explained. "I just keep track of the shipments, drive a forklift to move stuff around, you know. Whatever they need me to do."

Conner nodded. Was that what his father had taken off to do for the last eleven years? It was almost depressing.

"How 'bout you?" Mr. McDermott asked. "Do you have a job or . . . hobbies or something?"

"I write music," Conner said, lifting his chin slightly. People were usually impressed with that, but his father appeared unaffected.

"Country?" Mr. McDermott asked, raising his glass to indicate the speakers overhead, which were blaring out something extraordinarily twangy.

"Um, no," Conner said. "Rock, I guess you'd call it. I play guitar too."

His father gave him a blank stare. "I don't really listen to much music," he said.

Conner chewed on his lower lip and stared at the jukebox mounted on the side of the wall. *Well, this is going great,* he thought. After forty-five minutes together it still looked like the only thing he and his father had in common was old Fords.

"Can I get you anything else, Mikey?" the waitress asked as she passed by. She was a blond woman in her late twenties who had squeezed herself into a pair of tight, acid-wash jeans that were probably left over from her high-school days.

"You have any scotch back there, Vicki?" Mr. McDermott asked.

"You know we do," the waitress answered in a flirtatious tone. It was a little sickening, watching her act like that with his dad.

"Well, give me a glass of Glen Meringue on the rocks, then—none of that Dewar's stuff; it makes my throat burn."

Conner grinned appreciatively. Old Fords *and* good scotch—now they were getting somewhere. "Good choice," he told his father when Vicki arrived with the drink.

"You like scotch?" Mr. McDermott asked, a slight spark in his eye for the first time.

Conner nodded. "Especially the stuff off the top shelf," he said.

"Well, then," Mr. McDermott said. "Hey, Vicki!" he called. "Bring me another one of these, for my son here." He nodded toward Conner, and the waitress raised her eyebrows, as if she wasn't quite sure whether she believed Mike McDermott actually had a son or not. But she brought the drink anyway.

Ahhh, Conner thought, sipping the sour liquid. *Now, this is more like it.* He and his father both downed their drinks in under five minutes, and Mr. McDermott quickly ordered another round.

"You know," Conner said after a few swigs of his second scotch, "part of the reason I left El Carro was because Mom thought I had a drinking problem." He raised his glass and grinned at his father across the table.

Mr. McDermott laughed. "Sounds like your mom. She loved to overreact to things," he said. "You know, her father was an alcoholic—she's got a real hangup about that stuff."

"Huh," Conner said. He'd actually never known that about his grandfather, who'd died before he was born. It made sense, though—it wasn't just because of her own problem that his mom was always on his back about his drinking. It was because her father was a drunk too. No wonder she was so paranoid.

Conner polished off his second glass, noticing how the atmosphere in the bar felt a lot cozier now—warmer too. Alcohol was great for taking the edge off things—especially a good scotch.

"You want another?" Mr. McDermott asked, gesturing toward Conner's glass.

"Sure," Conner said. Who was he to turn down a free drink? When Vicki set the third scotch in front of him, Conner couldn't help but smirk. Coming to visit his father had definitely been the right thing to do. So what if the only interests they shared were drinking and cars? People got married with less in common.

In fact, he thought, *maybe I could even convince my father to let me stay with him—for good.*

Elizabeth held back a sigh as Evan pulled up in front of her house. She really hadn't wanted to come home tonight. After ditching the movie, they'd gone to the ice cream parlor in the mall and gotten another Mr. Wiggly Kiddie Surprise to split and then stopped in the arcade, where she'd beat Evan at every two-person video game they had played.

"I had a great time," she said, turning to face him.

"Me too," he agreed. He paused, glancing over at her house. "So . . . call me tomorrow if you need another distraction," he offered.

"Yeah, thanks," she said. She knew this was when she was supposed to get out of the car, but she couldn't bring herself to do it. Here, with Evan, she was safe. Safe from worrying about Conner, from Tia's anger or everyone else's pointless efforts to convince her that things would be fine when she knew they wouldn't be.

"So . . . ," she said, resting her fingers on the door handle.

"So . . . ," Evan echoed.

"So, maybe I'll see you tomorrow," she said. Evan nodded.

Time to get out, she told herself. She tried to turn the handle to open the door, but nothing happened. "I think it's stuck," she said, looking back at Evan.

"Oh, yeah, it does that sometimes," Evan said. "Try again."

She did, pushing her weight against the door, but it still didn't budge.

"I'll do it," Evan said, leaning closer and stretching his tan, muscular arm across her to grab the door handle. She was aware of the heat of his chest as it brushed against her shoulder, and suddenly her skin began to tingle.

He fiddled with the handle for a second, then the door sprang open.

"Thanks," she said, trying to keep her breathing steady.

"Sure," he said, slowly moving away. She felt his breath on her cheek as he pulled back toward his side of the car. He was so close—his mouth was only inches from hers. For a moment she could feel herself inch forward. She closed her eyes and leaned closer, realizing for the first time how much she wanted to kiss Evan. More than anything, she wanted to feel his arms wrapped tightly around her, the warmth of his touch. But when her lips brushed against Evan's, the reality of what she was about to do hit her.

"I can't," she blurted out, jumping back from him so fast that she practically fell out of the open door. "Evan, I—I'm sorry," she stammered awkwardly. "I have to go."

She ran across her front yard and stumbled into her house. What was the matter with her? Had she really been about to kiss one of Conner's best friends?

Yeah, she had. And the scariest part was that if Conner didn't come back soon, she wasn't sure *what* would happen next.

JEREMY AAMES

11:37 P.M.

The thing about Jade is that she's full of surprises. Just when I think I have a handle on things, she totally blindsides me—like with that card. I kind of feel like a jerk for not realizing she was actually serious about this whole anniversary thing. Maybe she really has changed. Maybe we don't have to keep things so casual. I should probably call her. No, it's too late. I can just talk to her in the morning. After her interview.

JADE WU
3:07 A.M.

Three A.M.? How did it get to be 3 A.M. so fast?

Oh, well. At least it's Sunday, so I can sleep in. It's not like I have anywhere to go. Or anyone to see. Or any boyfriend to call. I can sleep all day if I want.

CONNER MCDERMOTT
3:29 A.M.

After eleven years, my dad finally came through by giving me just what I needed—a good drink and a night without anybody on my case. I'd say that was worth the wait.

ELIZABETH WAKEFIELD

4:27 A.M.

I wonder if I'll ever sleep through the night again.